RIDING PASSION

Praise for D. Jackson Leigh

"*Call Me Softly* is a thrilling and enthralling novel of love, lies, intrigue and Southern charm."—*Bibliophilic Book Blog*

"D. Jackson Leigh understands the value of branding and delivers more of the familiar and welcome story elements that set her novels apart from other authors in the romance genre."—*The Rainbow Reader*

"Her prose is clean, lean, and mean—elegantly descriptive…"
—*Out in Print*

By the Author

Bareback

Long Shot

Call Me Softly

Touch Me Gently

Every Second Counts

Hold Me Forever

Dragon Horse War: The Calling

Riding Passion

Visit us at www.boldstrokesbooks.com

RIDING PASSION

by

D. Jackson Leigh

A Division of Bold Strokes Books

2015

ISBN 13: 978-1-62639-349-3

This Trade Paperback Original Is Published By
Bold Strokes Books, Inc.
P.O. Box 249
Valley Falls, NY 12185

First Edition: May 2015

Credits
Editor: Shelley Thrasher
Production Design: Stacia Seaman
Cover Design by Sheri (graphicartist2020@hotmail.com)

Acknowledgments

As always, I have to thank my awesome editor, Dr. Shelley Thrasher, for her continued patience and friendship. When I was reading through her edits and adding a few more of my own, I thought, "Whew! This is a lot of sex. Poor Shelley. She must have been shaking her head." So I added "First Kiss" to the mix to tone down the spice a bit. LOL. She didn't protest the late addition, so I took that as silent agreement. How she puts up with me, I don't know.

Also, a special shout-out to a hardworking group with whom I've spent some long, sweaty, wonderful days selling books at Pride events across the Southeast: Larkin Rose and her (awesome roadie) partner Rose, who started it all and I miss so much; the amazing Yolanda Wallace and partner (another loyal roadie) Dita; Donna K. Ford, puppy to my big dog, and her (very cool) partner Keah; the incomparable VK Powell; soft-spoken Erin Dutton and her partner (hey, look what I found) Chris; and, last but certainly not least, the Texan who stormed Atlanta Pride, Carsen Taite. Every one of them is such an inspiration to keep writing.

But those Pride events and very likely my writing career wouldn't be possible without the guidance and steadfast support of Len Barot and the entire Bold Strokes family. The professionalism and constant encouragement to improve is exactly the environment that suits this writer.

Finally, thanks to Radclyffe. When I saw her in P-town two years ago and said, "I'm thinking of putting together an anthology of my short stories," she shrugged and said, "Sure. Do it."

This book is dedicated to my readers.
There's nothing I enjoy more than meeting and talking with
people who, like me, like to read.

CONTENTS

DEAR READER

I know, I know. You saw the beautiful, intense woman on the cover of this book, and you're salivating over spending time with her. You will. She's my poet, Haze Baird, who finds her soul reflected in her cousin's neighbor, a mysterious artist, Sara Luna Espinosa de Lara. But, please, allow me a few moments of your time before you plunge in.

Riding Passion is an anthology—a D. Jackson Leigh sampler of sorts.

Half of the stories have been previously published in various anthologies by several presses, and I wanted to gather them in one place for you. Half of them are brand-new short stories.

Many of the stories revisit characters from my novels, and each is noted at the end of the story in the event you haven't read the book. Some other stories contain characters I'm considering for a novel-length tale later.

Warning: The heat rating ranges from very sweet ("First Kiss") to extra, extra spicy ("House of Memories" and "Surrender"). Wait! Don't automatically fast-forward to those last two just yet.

Riding Passion is more than a collection of short stories.

When I began writing the story of Haze and Luna, I couldn't seem to stop. So, their tale is actually a novella broken into three short segments. "Chasing Passion" introduces their story from Haze's point of view. "Riding Passion," the short story appropriately positioned at the pinnacle of the collection, continues their tale and clues you in to how Luna views their developing relationship. Then I take you back to Haze—leaving them and you—with "Passion's Bond" at the end of the collection.

I fell in love with these two characters and the free rein they gave me to explore and express a more formal and flowery writing style, much to the consternation of my editor. Fortunately for me, Shelley Thrasher has the patience of Job (she would mark that as a cliché) and, hopefully like my readers, will sometimes indulge me.

I hope you enjoy the ride,

D. Jackson Leigh

Chasing Passion

Haze

She was a whisper of mist in the moonlight.

The rain had finally let up and the clouds cleared so the half moon illuminated my path to the cliff's edge. I'd taken up residence at Ravencroft only a bare two months before, but the flat ledge overlooking the Pacific had quickly become my favorite refuge, my port of calm in the storm that was my life.

Fingers of warm, damp fog that rose from the rolling ocean to caress the strip of sandy beach seemed to reach for her as she cantered into my world on a white stallion. The instant I saw her, the night grew warmer, the wind breathed deeper, and the ocean tides pulled stronger. Everything—the rocks at the foot of the cliff, the muffled sound of hooves on the wet sand, the ever-changing waterline—came into sharp focus under the muted light.

At first, I thought her an apparition, a strange wisp of fog forming in the sometimes-deceptive moon glow. Her long, pale hair rippled in the coastal winds like shining waves, like the silk of my shirt billowing against my heated skin. Were it not for the contrasting tanned skin of her bare limbs, I would have been convinced.

She sat her steed bareback, in perfect relaxed ease. Wind plastered the white, gauzy tunic against her breasts and pushed the loose sleeves up to expose slender, golden forearms. From that distance, I could only imagine long-fingered hands expertly grasping the reins that mastered her beast. My own hands twitched at the impulse to hold those imagined fingers to measure their length and heat and texture. Her loose trousers fluttered against the stallion's firm flank. Did she have a closet full of white linen pants so she needn't worry that the ones she wore would be permanently stained by horse sweat and sea brine? Her feet were bare, obviously because such an angel need not actually touch the harsh mortal landscape.

My mare nickered quietly, her ears pricked forward, and I wrapped my hand around her nose to stop her from calling out to the other horse. The fingers of fog became a hand and reclaimed the stallion and his mistress, pulling them back into the shrouded night.

I passed much of the next two weeks on that ledge, hoping for another glimpse of her. Full moon came and went as I fruitlessly searched for her in the waning lunar cycle. When the night became too dark, I rose before sunrise and searched for her in the morning mists. I spent entire afternoons scanning the beach with my binoculars.

As the first week gave way to a second, I began to pass my vigil with pad and pen, finding my voice for the first time since my life had erupted in a maelstrom several months before. I penned line after line of poetry from my heart to my mysterious rider.

Near the end of the fortnight, I was sitting cross-legged on the sun-warmed ledge, head bent to my work, when the soft sound of hooves on hard-packed sand pulled me from my musings. I fumbled with my binoculars and was scrambling to my feet when my mare, Rika, called to the stallion below.

I'd begun to think I'd imagined her, so I grasped a measure of jeans and flesh and pinched to test my current reality. Ow. I wasn't dreaming.

Rika, slut that she was, called again. The stallion slowed and turned toward my lookout, then raised his head and issued a throaty answering neigh.

Even more beautiful in daylight, she wore a form-fitting white tank and linen shorts, dressed to capture the afternoon sun. Instead, she captured me.

My skin prickled—my binoculars unnecessary and forgotten—as her face lifted. Our eyes locked and held, though her stallion danced impatiently. She tilted her head in question. Or was it invitation?

I stood stunned, like a shy adolescent, before finally raising my hand in a weak wave. She smiled, amusement dancing across her features, then wheeled her stallion and galloped in the direction they'd come.

"Wait." My shout fell uselessly onto the beach. "I wanted to talk to you," I murmured to myself.

I scanned the cliff below, frantic for a path that would lead down to the beach. Why hadn't I thought of this before? Like an idiot, I'd wasted hours, days, nights, writing haunted, longing verse without practical thought as to how I would intercept her. This disconnect between my world and reality was exactly what had me hiding out at Ravencroft now.

I was still admonishing myself when I saw it. The hacienda blended so well into the landscape I would have missed it if the sun hadn't kissed a window to wink back at me. Was that her castle, her lair, her haven? I moved to the edge of my lookout, but the sandy strand below was empty. How could she have vanished? I grabbed my binoculars but could see no breach in the stone cliff, no path traveling down from my perch or up to the newly discovered residence.

Disgusted with my lack of planning, I stomped around my ledge to gather my things and then flung myself onto Rika's back to return to Ravencroft so I could wander the joyless rooms and wallow in my dark mood.

❖

My mood was still black as two mornings later I dished out grain to the stable of eight horses. I'd spent the previous day riding trails throughout my cousin's estate in search of a path to the shore. I was convinced that none existed.

I sighed as my scoop scraped the bottom of the last grain barrel. Instructions were tacked on the wall of the feed room. With only a phone call I could have more grain delivered, but I'd been craving something fresh from the fish market. And, much to my surprise, I finally was tired of my own company after rattling around the huge house alone for months of restless days and sleepless nights.

My cousin, Dante, and his partner were on an extended holiday in Europe, and needing to lay low for a while, I had agreed to be mistress of the manor in their absence. Shortly after they departed, the man who minded their stable was injured in a car accident. He was recovering, but it left the chore of feeding horses and cleaning stalls to me. Dante's man had recommended a temporary replacement, but I found the physical labor a welcome respite from sulking over the situation I had fled on the East Coast.

A quick survey of my attire confirmed that the morning feeding hadn't soiled my jeans and black polo. My knee-length riding boots were dusty, but good enough for the open market and the feed store. So, I retrieved my wallet from the house and hopped into Dante's Land Rover.

I ordered most of my groceries online from an upscale market on the edge of town because they delivered and spared me the drudgery of the curious public. So, no one knew of my presence here except the injured groom, who was sworn to secrecy. And, although Dante had assured me the locals were very good at keeping secrets to protect the serenity of their little seaside town, I worried I was risking a leak that would bring a horde of paparazzi to my doorstep. Still, the prospect of human contact and my burning need for information overruled my fears, so I pulled my shoulder-length hair through my ball cap as I snugged it low on my head and donned dark sunglasses.

Feed stores are notorious centers of gossip. I've never visited one that didn't have a small seating area where a requisite handful of retired locals gathered to keep an eye on the door and eavesdrop on conversations. This store was no different. It was nearly time for them to adjourn to their homes for lunch, but two men—one grizzled with a two-day-old beard and the other neat in his pressed flannel shirt—lingered in the mismatched collection of chairs grouped next to the store's large front window.

I nodded to them as I strode to the counter to address the middle-aged man leaning on the cash register. "I need to put in a grain order for Ravencroft," I said.

He nodded. "Tom's overdue for a delivery, but I expect his broke leg has things a bit off schedule up there. You want the usual order?"

"Uh, yeah. Whatever Tom usually gets."

"I've got another delivery going up that way in the morning. That soon enough?"

"Tomorrow will be fine if I can get a bag to take with me for tonight's feed." I was surprised that he didn't seem at all curious about me, so I stuck out my hand. "I'm Haze, Dante's cousin. I'm looking after the place while he's gallivanting around Europe for four months."

His handshake was firm. "Rob Carter. I heard you'd turned down Tom's offer to find somebody to fill in until he was on his feet again."

I glanced at our audience of two, who were listening to every word, and frowned. If these guys knew, then half the town probably was aware that Dante's disgraced cousin was holed up at Ravencroft. Rob seemed to read my mind.

"Tom had to tell his wife so she could let you know he was in the hospital and wouldn't show up to feed the next morning."

Ah, the woman who'd called to explain about Tom's accident. It obviously couldn't be helped, but I scowled nonetheless.

Rob shrugged. "Well, as tight-lipped as Tom is, telling

Esmie's as good as broadcasting it on the nightly news." His clear, blue eyes met mine. "Hope it hasn't caused any problems for you."

I blinked at him, unsure why he'd even care. "Nobody's been bothering me."

"Good."

"And I'd like to keep it that way."

"We like to keep things quiet around here, too," the grizzled eavesdropper said.

I wasn't sure if his warning was for the paparazzi or me.

"If they come looking, even Esmie will clam up. We don't take to strangers much." The neat old man's tone was gentle but firm. "Who you've been knocking boots with isn't any of our concern, unless you're looking to stir the same pot around here."

I wasn't. Wait. Maybe I was. This was awkward. I couldn't exactly ask questions about my mystery woman now. Irritated at my dilemma, I scribbled my signature on the receipt Rob plunked down on the counter. "I'll wait outside for the bag of grain," I said.

I was propped against the side of the Rover, kicking the dusty gravel of the parking lot, when Rob appeared with fifty pounds of sweet feed slung over his shoulder. He expertly flipped it into the back of the vehicle and I slammed the tailgate closed.

"Don't take offense at those two old codgers. They didn't mean to put you off. They're both widowers and don't have anything else to occupy them. They're in there now arguing over how tall you are and whether you look like a poet."

She didn't even know him and shouldn't care what he thought, but she was tired of not defending herself. "For what it's worth, I'm innocent. I didn't have an affair with the first lady. We're friends. The president's political enemies fabricated the rest. It's made my life hell."

"Well, sir," he said quietly. "I can't imagine what that must be like, but nobody's gonna hear from me that you're here." He grimaced. "Except...I guess I did tell one person."

I frowned at him, narrowing my eyes.

"Luna. She was curious about who was visiting Dante. She's your neighbor to the south, so I figured it was okay."

"To the south?" My mind was instantly a big compass I was fumbling to calibrate…sun sets in the west, so— "Does she ride a white Andalusian?" I had an eye for the old breeds, and I'd often been accused of preferring horses to people. So it surprised me a bit that I'd barely noticed her magnificent stallion. Outside my career as a lauded poet, breeding horses at my Maryland farm was my passion.

"That would be her. You only missed her by a few minutes."

Luna. Her name was beautiful, too. "I've seen her riding on the beach." I shook his hand again. "Don't worry about it. Have a good day."

"Can't get any better," he said, smiling. "It's unusual for her to come by instead of her foreman. Two attractive women in one day. If it keeps up, I'm going to start charging those old codgers admission so they can gawk."

He climbed the steps to the store's front platform but turned when I called out to him. "Yeah?"

"Six-two. Tell the old guys I'm six feet, two inches tall."

He laughed and waved before ducking into the doorway.

As I drove a few blocks to the open market, I was both elated she'd inquired about me and disappointed that I'd missed meeting her. I'd almost decided against the market, fighting the urge to rush home and saddle Rika for a ride to the neighboring estate. But I didn't even know her. And, I was hiding out because of another woman. Did I really want to tempt fate this soon?

This was silly. I'd only seen the woman from a distance, and she was filling my every thought. On the other hand, she had me once again filling my notebook with verse. Yes, no. I want her. I shouldn't. I shook my head to clear it and parked the Rover.

I selected a sea bass from the fishmonger's display and stared absently down the vendor-lined lane while he filleted it for me. I froze. A woman stood outside an art gallery, talking to a man in the doorway. Her blond hair rippled like spun silk against her shoulder blades. She was dressed like I was, in jeans and calf-length boots, but her blouse was the color of the blood moon, loose, with the long sleeves rolled up onto her forearms. I could hardly tear my eyes from her well-shaped hips and long legs. Was it really her? I wasn't certain without white linen against tanned skin. Without a massive stallion nearby. I willed her to turn around so I could see her face.

"Miss? Your fish?"

I took my package and practically threw a couple of bills at him. "Keep the change," I said absently.

When I turned back to the street, I glimpsed her profile as she handed over a canvas from an open Jeep parked nearby and then climbed in and drove in the opposite direction. Damn, damn, damn. Missed her again.

After hurriedly selecting produce from another vendor, I barely restrained myself from breaking into a trot as I headed for the gallery. The store was narrow, and its walls were covered from floor to ceiling with paintings of every size and subject. A few racks of less-expensive numbered prints for tourists stood near the door. The shopkeeper was nowhere in sight, but I heard someone rummaging in the loft at the back of the store.

"Hello?"

The man I'd seen take her canvas leaned out over the railing. "Up here. I'll be down in five minutes if you aren't in a hurry."

"Take your time. I can browse while I wait." I didn't want to appear too eager.

I pocketed my sunglasses and shook my hair free of the ball cap to take full advantage of the store's air-conditioning.

As expected, seascapes and landscapes dominated his displays, but I was drawn toward the rear of the store where the back wall was covered by paintings from the same artist. The signature was simply "L.E." The strokes and texture of the works fascinated me. Their subjects ranged widely, from local scenes around town to a pair of fighting stallions to portraits of women.

One had a decidedly lesbian feel. A woman lounged nude in a window seat, smirking at the artist as a burning cigarette dangled in her fingers.

"That artist is amazing, isn't she?"

I wasn't startled because I'd heard him clumping down the stairs toward me. "Yes." I touched the initials on the painting of the horses. "L.E.?"

"Luna Espinosa. Her paintings mostly sell in the New York and L.A. galleries. The only reason I have any of her work is because she lives in the area." He removed a painting by another artist and set it aside. "She was just here, dropping off this new piece, already framed. When you came in, I was adding a wire so I could hang it." He hung a two-by-three foot painting in place of the one he'd removed.

I *was* startled by the seascape. If you stared hard enough, the waves seemed to almost move as they reached for the trail of hoof prints along the narrow strip of sand that ribboned between sea and crag. A figure stood at the top of the cliff, the face an indistinct shadow under a full moon. Still, heat rose from my chest and burned my neck. It was easy enough to recognize my brown hair whipping and silk shirt billowing in the night winds. My gaze slid to the bottom corner. This painting was titled. "Night Watcher." L.E.

"How much?"

"Uh, well." He scratched his head. "I'm not sure it's for sale. She said she'd give me a thousand-dollar commission to display it and call her if anyone inquired about it."

"I'm inquiring. Call her." That painting was meant for me. I was sure of it. "I'll double your commission to phone her now."

"She's probably not home yet."

"You have her cell number, don't you?"

"Sure, but—" He shifted uncomfortably under my glare and nervously picked up the painting he'd just taken down.

I pulled my wallet from my pocket and waved my no-limit American Express at him. "Tell her to name her price."

"I'll see if I can get in touch with her." He disappeared into an office but left the door ajar.

I stared at the painting. She'd been watching me watch her. I felt like a child caught doing something embarrassing, except I was glad to be discovered. She'd noticed something intimate I didn't let others see: a part of me that wasn't poised and aloof, but desperate and desiring. Pressure built low in my belly and my flesh pebbled.

When he didn't immediately return, I edged toward the partially open door to eavesdrop.

"She's insistent…Yes, a woman…I don't know. I didn't ask her name. Should I recognize her?…Uh, tall, shoulder-length brown hair, blond highlights. Oh, and sort of striking green eyes…Wearing?…Yeah, riding boots like you…Are you sure?… Okay. It's your money."

I hurried back to the painting as quietly as my hard-soled boots would allow and struck a casual pose as if I hadn't moved.

"The painting is yours." He took it from the wall and began wrapping it in thick brown paper while my card was processing. "A thousand bucks."

"Excuse me?"

"Your half of the commission." He glanced at my name on the card and eyed me as though seeing me for the first time. "She said there was no charge for the painting."

❖

I drove back to Ravencroft, gloating over my prize. I'd captured a piece of her. Not exactly captured, because she'd given it to me. Even better.

I unloaded my bounty but left it covered in the thick brown protective paper to prolong my anticipation while I prepared and ate my lunch. By the time I'd eaten the last bite and cleaned the last dish, I wanted to rip and tear the paper away.

Instead, I carefully removed the wrapping and studied the

painting at length, trying to interpret how she saw me. My stance was spread to brace against the wind, one arm raised to brush back a strand of hair lashing at my cheek. My posture was bold, not clandestine. I was relieved that she apparently didn't view me as threatening.

I pursed my lips. Where to hang it? I actually spent little time in the house. I was usually at the stable or my watch ledge, or reading and writing on the terrace. I couldn't hang it in any of those places. While I mulled my dilemma, I turned the picture around to ensure the hanging wire was secure.

What's this? A map was carefully inked on the back. So that's how she got down to the beach. "Low tide" was written next to the drawing. I scrambled for my computer and found a tide chart for the area. Not until eight o'clock tonight. An eternity.

❖

The long, interminable hours until low tide had nearly undone me, but I was at last mounted. The moon was nearly full again and the forest sparse enough that the trail was sufficiently illuminated.

Her secret was a tunnel through the rock. Fewer than ten yards long, it dipped in the middle so that high tide nearly filled it and prevented passage to anyone other than a swimmer. Low tide opened a passageway about four feet wide and less than twelve feet high. The moon reached down into the cavern and glinted off the shallow puddle at its apex. The roof was so close in several places, I had to duck low over my mare's neck and was relieved that Rika didn't try to jump the puddle and leave my brains and hers on the rock overhead.

I emerged onto the beach and into the painting. The ocean licked at the strip of sand marked by a line of hoof prints that led north. I followed, laying a second line of indentions alongside hers. Not a watcher but a tracker now.

I had gone but a hundred yards when Rika sniffed the wind

and whinnied into the night. My skin prickled, and the hair on the back of my neck rose in warning. I peered ahead but saw only the trail I was following. Then, recognizing a jetty of rock that disappeared into the surf, I looked up at my own watch ledge. Not tracker but prey.

She smiled down at me and raised her hand in a casual wave, then pushed it toward me, palm out. Stay.

Her game both intrigued and annoyed me. I'd spent the last months a political victim and, despite my fascination with her, wasn't willing to be her toy. While I waited, I cantered my mare in a wide circle, then a series of figure eights to keep rein on my impatience. And when she emerged from the tunnel, I galloped boldly toward her.

We met and circled, each measuring the other. She was even more beautiful than I'd anticipated, dressed in the same white linen tunic and pants as the first time I saw her. Although she was astride in saddle tonight, her feet were bare as before.

"You're the poet," she said. "The first lady's suitor."

Her voice was a lush melody on the sea breeze, neither throaty nor girlish, but her words were needles prickling my skin, my pride. I glared at her wordlessly.

She cocked her head, her expression surprised. "I meant no offense. Only admiration."

I averted my gaze, staring down at the reins in my hand, and cursed my runaway life. "Your compliment is undeserved. I didn't…I don't want to talk about that." I broke our circular dance and guided Rika toward the tunnel. "If you wanted to meet only to satisfy your curiosity, you can read the newspapers."

Her stallion easily caught up with my mare. Her hand was as I imagined, long-fingered and soft as it lay on my fist that clenched the reins. "Wait. Please."

I reined Rika to a stop, not because of her request but because, despite my temper, I despaired at leaving her.

"Stay." She trailed her hand up my forearm and squeezed. "I don't care about what brought you here." She circled around so that we were mane to tail, knees nearly touching. She brushed her fingers along my thigh. "I want to know the woman who stands watch day and night, so bold and handsome." She raised her hand to caress my jaw. "I want to experience the poet who sits on her sunny ledge and scribbles her heart, her emotions in lines of verse."

Lamb to the slaughter. I wanted to resist for the sake of propriety, to prop up my pride. But Luna in the moonlight was magical and I was bewitched.

"Please, come have a drink with me?"

"Yes, okay." While my reply was simple, the vortex of emotions swirling around it was not.

I followed her through the tunnel and shadowed woods, feeling a bit like Alice braving the rabbit hole. We emerged at a sprawling Spanish hacienda, and a boy ran up to us, face flushed and worshipful eyes pinned to Luna as we dismounted. After a few words of rapid Spanish, he led our horses away, and I despaired that I might display the same starstruck visage.

It was Luna, however, who couldn't seem to tear her eyes from my face as she offered her hand in belated introduction.

"I am Sara Luna Espinosa de Lara. Welcome to my home."

I cocked my head at her earnest introduction. Did she really think I didn't know who she was and of her standing in the art world? I felt the advantage tilt my way and grabbed it with both hands as I bent to kiss the back of hers. "Haze Baird, at your service."

Amusement illuminated her features at my romantically formal gesture. "You may want to qualify that."

Still partially bent over her hand, I smiled. "I have no restrictions when it comes to beautiful women." I hesitated, my past predicament abruptly stabbing into my present. "Unless they're already claimed by another, of course." I straightened and held her gaze. "I never, *ever* encroach."

Her dark eyes shone like her name. "Then there's no problem here. I'm no one's claim." Her gaze wandered over my features and down my body. She was at least five-ten, but I still bested her height. She picked up my hands and examined them. "I want to draw your hands," she murmured. She traced my jaw with her fingers. "And you have a face that begs to be on canvas." She nodded as if it was decided and I'd given my consent—which I guess I had when I said no restrictions. She gestured to a table where a cluster of candles flickered next to a cut-crystal decanter, two glasses, and a plate of small pastries.

We sat and she poured two snifters and offered one to me. "I distill my own amaretto," she said.

I swirled it under my nose—sweet and thick and almond scented—and then took it on my tongue. I nodded silently and bit into a pecan-encrusted pastry before taking another sip. I chewed and sipped again. With her eyes intent upon my mouth, I slowly licked an imagined drop from my lips. "The combination of pecan and marzipan with the almond liquor is decadent," I said, holding up the remaining half of the pastry. "Would you like to taste?"

Her lips lingered when she stole the sweet from my fingers and held my gaze while she chewed. When she lifted her snifter, she offered the cordial to me instead. I drank from it and she moved close, her lips sampling mine before her tongue plunged past to glean the sweet liquor from the recesses of my mouth.

This is when propriety and restraint should have prevailed. We had only formally introduced ourselves moments before.

Instead, I groaned and grasped her nape with one hand and the small of her back with the other so that when I stood, she came with me and our bodies pressed together. I cursed the silk of my shirt and the linen of her tunic that separated us.

She disengaged but didn't desert. Her eyes searched mine, and when she spoke, I felt her warm breath riding each word. "I don't jump into bed right after meeting somebody."

"It's okay." I caressed her cheek with mine and slipped my hands under her tunic. I was dizzy with the need to have her skin, her breasts against mine. "I don't either."

"That's good," she said, unbuttoning my shirt to push her hands inside the black silk and cup my small breasts. She thumbed my rigid nipples.

"Luna." Intended to be a warning, her name sounded like a plea.

"Come," she said, grabbing my hand and pulling me into the house.

We stood beside the huge bed in a room the size of Ravencroft's living room. Huge windows opened to the soothing sounds and scent of the ocean. I lifted her gauzy tunic from her long torso, and my breath caught when the moon kissed the smooth skin of her shoulders and teased her pebbled nipples. She smelled of sea and coconut, tasted of sweet almonds and faint brine.

She let me taste and touch but a moment. "Off," she said, yanking my shirt from my jeans and off my shoulders. My arms held captive in my shirt, she rubbed her full breasts against mine and we both moaned. "Undress, but don't move," she ordered me.

I disrobed while she circled and examined me with an artist's eye. She murmured to herself in Spanish as she cupped the curve of my breast, stroked the crest of my shoulder, and measured the V of my back with her hands. She clucked at a scar on my buttock and slid to her knees in front of me to squeeze my hard thighs.

My need throbbed, and I instinctively widened my stance to relieve it. She looked up, her face inches from my sex, her eyes and nostrils flaring. I thought, hoped, she would take me as she knelt. Instead, she stood. "I want to sketch you," she said.

"Later." I reached for her, but she dodged away.

"Just a quick one. I need to capture my first impression." She'd already grabbed the sketchpad from the bedside table.

I crossed my arms over my chest. "Not unless you strip first."

She stopped, her pencil in midair.

"Or I'll dress and leave right now."

Her eyes glinted and her mouth curved in a half smile. She

tossed the pad onto the bed and dropped her pants to the floor before kicking them away. I wondered again at her propensity for white and her disregard for how easily it is soiled.

She was gorgeous. No tan lines, her bronzed skin was natural. The golden hue of her hair was not, but I considered it adornment rather than pretense. More interesting were the tribal tattoos that bracketed her hips and arrowed toward her center.

I'd insisted that she bare herself to even the balance of vulnerability, but she wore her nakedness like she'd been freed rather than exposed. I was helpless to tear my eyes from the curve of her hips, the slope of her belly, the dusk of her nipples as she circled like a dancer, defining me with sure, confident strokes of her pencil.

Though the night was mild, sweat trickled down my neck and between my breasts. I struggled to relax in the bindings of her request to pose, but my rebellious body quickened at the restraint. Heat rose in my belly and seared through my chest. Arousal wet my thighs. When she at last looked up from her sketching and met my eyes, she gasped. She clearly could see my hunger, my burning need for her.

Before she fully placed her drawing on the table I had her in my arms, then on the bed. I pinned her beneath me so my angel couldn't flee, and I ravished her with tongue and teeth and kisses so she wouldn't want to fly away.

I kissed my way down her belly and shouldered between her thighs, ravenous for a taste of her, starving for her sweet moans. I licked her with eager strokes, then took her in my mouth and sucked her swelling tissues. And when her breath hitched with her impending orgasm, I thrust my fingers into her.

She came for me. Her legs tightened around my ears, shutting out everything but my heart thudding in time with the pulsing of her sex. Her cries were a lyrical verse, and with my fingers inside her, still stroking, I surged forward, my groans an alliteration. I slicked her golden thigh, chasing, seeking a couplet of pleasure.

"Luna, Luna."

Each thrust of my hips swelled my pleasure and thrust my fingers deep inside her. She tightened again.

"Haze." My name was a breathy exhalation. "Oh, God, I'm going to come again."

Hanging on to the edge with her, I felt my belly clench for release. "Do it. Come with me."

I thrust, again and again, my hips jerking hard with urgency.

My shout and her cry were a loud haiku, my shudders and her whimpers the closing refrain.

I withdrew slowly and licked her from my fingers, her eyes glinting in the soft light as she watched. Then I rolled onto my back and pulled her close.

"Stay," she murmured, her head resting on my shoulder.

"Yes," I answered, my tortured soul finally at rest under a soothing blanket of moonlight and Luna.

THE PORTRAIT

"I swear I never saw it coming. Sure, things haven't been that good in the bedroom for us in a while, but I've been building a business and I had surgery and my sister was sick—"

"And your dog died, your daddy went to prison, and your mama got run over by a train." Mick finished her friend Diane's litany of woes.

Diane looked up from the designs she was drawing in her refried beans. "Asshole."

Mick and Diane had been friends since college, but enough was enough. "It's been a year, buddy. You need to get over Cheryl." Mick softened her voice. "Have you thought about seeing someone professionally to talk about it?"

"Go see a shrink? Hell no." Diane threw her napkin onto her plate. "Didn't know I was being a nuisance. I'll shut up about it."

"Come on, I'm serious. This is…what…your sixth live-in relationship? Maybe it wouldn't hurt to figure out what you're doing wrong…whether it's picking the wrong women or leaving the cap off the toothpaste."

"So, you finally admit that you think it was my fault."

"Listen to yourself, Diane. You're the one who said Cheryl tried to tell you she was unhappy. All she wanted was for you to—"

"The only thing I did wrong with Cheryl was believe her

when she said that young bitch hanging around her was just a friend."

As much as she loved her buddy, Mick had listened to the same tirade a million times.

Diane stopped and narrowed her eyes at Mick's impatient sigh. "Maybe you should listen to yourself for a change."

"What are you talking about?" Mick said.

"I'm talking about your new neighbor, the hot young artist who's been hovering around Sophie for the past two months."

Mick slid forward in her chair and pointed a finger at Diane. "Don't even go there. I trust Sophie completely."

"Uh-huh. How much time have you spent with her lately?"

"I'm an accountant and we just finished tax season. We've been together almost twenty-five years. Sophie knows what tax season is like by now."

"Bet Miss Hottie doesn't have to worry about tax season."

Mick stood. "I know you're still hurt over Cheryl. That's the only reason I'm not going to punch your lights out and tell Sophie what you've insinuated about her." She threw some money on the table to pay for her lunch. "Get some help, Diane."

❖

Mick studied her reflection in the plate glass that was the back wall of her fifth-floor office. When had those lines appeared around her mouth? Sophie said they were frown lines. Mick raised the corners of her mouth to make them disappear, but her smile looked more like a grimace and accentuated the crow's-feet around her eyes. She'd considered dying her short, spiky hair when it turned snow white, but Sophie refused. It was the perfect contrast to Mick's blue eyes, she insisted.

Mick still felt the same as she did when she was thirty. But the person looking back at her was old. Too old to have a lover fifteen years younger. Despite her adamant rejection of Diane's implication, the seed of doubt had been planted, its roots taking hold in Mick's thoughts all afternoon.

She sighed and turned away from her introspection. It was only four o'clock, but Sophie had warned her not to be late coming home tonight. It was Mick's sixtieth birthday. Damn it. She didn't want to have another birthday. She wanted time to stand still for her but let Sophie catch up. She wanted to be the gracious one, the one to laugh and say, I love every line in your face. At least she'd talked Sophie out of throwing a big party like she did for Mick's fiftieth.

She started to toss a few files into her briefcase, then thought better of it. No taking work home tonight. And, damn it, she'd use the stairs this time. Old, out-of-shape people rode the elevator. She grabbed her keys and punched the office intercom.

"Rachel, I'm gone for the day…going out the back way."

"I'll call Sophie so she'll have time to chase the naked women out of the house." The receptionist's standard reply was an old joke from the time Sophie had to teach a body-sculpture class in her home studio because the college wouldn't allow nude models. Mick usually laughed, but today the quip settled like soured milk on her stomach.

I'm talking about that new neighbor you have, the hot young artist who's been hovering around Sophie for the past two months.

Mick shook the thought from her head. That was just stupid. She pushed the door open and headed for the Toyota in her reserved parking space. Maybe she'd go car shopping this weekend and buy that BMW convertible she'd always wanted. Yeah. Why not? A present to herself. They could afford it. Her mood suddenly lighter, Mick revved up the Camry, turned off the air-conditioner, and rolled the windows down. It wasn't a convertible, but the wind blowing through her hair felt satisfyingly reckless.

❖

Mick breezed through the house with a grin on her face. It was her birthday, after all, and she planned to cash in on that. Her. Sophie. Naked.

Her smile disappeared when she pushed open the door to the studio. Sophie wasn't alone. Garrett, the studly artist who'd recently moved next door, huddled close as they murmured over something in Sophie's sketchbook.

"What's so interesting?" Mick growled.

Sophie slapped the sketchbook shut and stood. "Hey, honey. You're early, aren't you?"

Mick pulled Sophie to her, pressed their hips together, and kissed her possessively. "It's my birthday. I get anything I want on my birthday, right? That includes coming home early and ravishing my sexy wife, doesn't it?"

Sophie glanced at Garrett and laughed nervously, pushing against Mick's shoulders. "Slow down, tiger. Garrett needs a favor before you start unwrapping birthday gifts."

Garrett gave Sophie a conspiratorial look. "I apologize for delaying your birthday plans, but we're only talking about a few minutes."

Mick frowned. Exactly what was she implying would take only a few minutes, the favor or Mick's seduction?

"Go on," Sophie said. "Garrett can't figure out the controls on the whirlpool tub, and I need to get cleaned up before we can go to dinner."

Mick moved her hands down and gave Sophie's butt a squeeze. "When I get back, we'll review what's on the menu."

Sophie blushed and glanced over at Garrett again. "I need at least twenty minutes to get ready."

❖

Mick impatiently followed as Garrett casually sauntered to the house next door. The brick, Tudor-style house was a third larger than her and Sophie's house. Garrett had moved in two months before and quickly bonded with Sophie when they realized they were both artists.

"So, I know you're an artist, but how do you make your living? Do you teach somewhere like Sophie?" Surely Garrett had some young students who were more interesting than Mick's wife.

"No. I seriously doubt I'd have the patience for teaching. I paint portraits."

"Really. Sophie hates painting portraits. Says it's too boring."

Garrett turned to Mick and smiled. "I suppose a lot of people think that. I like the challenge of finding that characteristic that makes each individual unique and figuring out how to make it shine through in the painting."

"I'm not sure what you mean."

"Like a 'tell' gives away what someone's thinking during a poker game. Let me see if I can come up with a good example." Garrett was silent as she led Mick upstairs to the extravagant bathroom of the master suite and turned toward the huge mirror over the double vanity. "A mentor pointed out to me that I tend to talk with my body more than most people…the set of my shoulders is indicative of my mood, I cock my head when I'm thinking, tuck my chin and look up through my eyelashes when I'm aroused, thrust my chin out when I feel threatened. A good portrait painter should be able to capture that."

Could this woman be more self-absorbed?

Garrett gestured toward the mirror. "What about yourself? What would someone need to see to paint you effectively?"

Mick shrugged as she surveyed the pinstripes in her white shirt that matched her neatly pressed black Dockers. "I just see me. I don't spend a lot of time looking at myself in the mirror." Technically, the window in her office wasn't a mirror.

Garrett chuckled. "A necessity of my occupation, I'm afraid." She eyed Mick. "Okay. Let's try someone you do look at often. Sophie's tell is her lips. She purses her lips when she's thinking. She pokes them out in a pout when she's not happy. She chews her bottom lip when she's nervous. She stretches them in a thin line when she's pissed."

"You've been looking at my wife's lips?"

"Down, girl. As a professional portrait painter, I can't help noticing things about almost everyone I spend time around."

Mick didn't want to think about how much time Garrett had been spending with Sophie. She wanted to be done with this pesky neighbor, go home and lay clear claim to her wife. "You needed help with the whirlpool?"

Garrett pressed the buttons on the tub's controls. Not a ripple in the water. "I called the Realtor and she said everything was inspected before the sale. I checked the breaker in the fuse box and it's definitely in the 'on' position. Sophie said you helped the previous owner with the same problem, but she couldn't remember what you did to fix it."

"There's a safety cutoff in the bedroom closet that keeps you from accidentally turning the jets on and burning up the pump when there's no water. They probably switched it off when they drained the tub to inspect it before you closed on the house."

Mick went to the closet and flipped the switch, then returned to the bathroom to punch the control. The water churned.

"Great! Thanks, Mick."

"Not a problem. Planning to share this tub with someone special?" Like a young, sexy girlfriend who wasn't already in a committed partnership next door.

"Nope. Just me and my sore back."

Mick didn't care about Garrett's sore back. "Well, I've got a hot date with more than a tub tonight, and I don't want to keep her waiting."

"Let me at least offer you a beer for helping me out. Sophie said you're something of a beer connoisseur, and I have some great dark ales."

"Maybe some other time."

❖

Mick hurried back and quietly let herself into the house. She was hoping to surprise Sophie in mid-dress so she wouldn't fuss about ruining her makeup when Mick tossed her on the bed and cashed in on her birthday. She'd show her that this sixty-year-old could still serve up hot, monkey sex. She didn't need some young stud from next door. But as she approached their bedroom, she heard Sophie talking in a low voice.

"No, it's fine. I don't think she noticed and I've got it covered up now. Thanks, Garrett. That was smart of you to plan ahead for a distraction if she ever caught us by surprise. I know. Soon. I wanted to, before her birthday, but I need more time. Thank you for being so patient. This means so much to me. I know. Bye."

Mick's stomach churned. What was Sophie covering up? They never kept secrets from each other. What was Garrett being patient about? It was pretty obvious, wasn't it? Diane was right. Something was going on, and Garrett wanted Sophie to admit it to Mick.

Her biggest fear, the one buried so deep even she hadn't realized she harbored it, was that at some point the gap between their ages would make a difference. When had she become sixty and boring? Sophie was a young forty-five. When she hit seventy, Sophie would be a very datable fifty-five. After nearly twenty-five years together, their time was coming to an end.

Her vision swam, and she caught herself against the wall as her knees buckled. God, she was going to pass out. She whirled and stumbled down the hall, crashing into a table in the foyer. The sculpture she gave Sophie for their tenth anniversary crashed to the floor, shattering along with Mick's life.

"Mick! Honey, are you okay?"

Mick steadied herself against the wall and stared down at the pieces of sculpture scattered across the Italian tile. She jerked away when Sophie reached for her hand. "I heard you." She choked on the words, her voice only a hoarse whisper.

Sophie froze. "You heard what?"

Mick stepped over the mess to put some distance between

her and Sophie. She crossed her arms tightly over her chest, trying desperately to hold the shards of her heart together. "I heard you talking to that neighborhood Romeo, the one who's over here every time I call home from work. The one you were cuddled up with in your studio when I got home today. The one you were just whispering to on the phone." Her hurt, her anger, her voice rose with each sentence.

"Neighborhood Romeo?" Sophie threw back her head and laughed.

To Mick's dismay, her eyes filled with tears. The Sophie she knew would never be so callous. Had she changed this much while Mick had her head buried in tax returns?

She clenched her jaw against the sob that was rising in her throat. Garrett might have stolen her wife, but Mick wouldn't surrender her dignity, too. She jammed her hands in her pockets, her fingers finding her car keys. She had to get away. She turned and strode through the house toward the garage. She made it to the kitchen before Sophie nearly tackled her, wrapping her arms tight around Mick from behind.

"Mick, sweetheart, slow down. Wait."

"I can't…I can't do this."

"Oh my God. You're shaking."

Sophie loosened her hold to slip in front of Mick and gaze up at her. Mick stared at the floor, afraid of what she'd see if she looked into Sophie's dark-chocolate eyes. Sophie gave her a little shake. Her voice was soft. "Michelle Louise Sanderson. I'd smack you if you weren't so seriously upset. First of all, I was not cuddled up with Garrett. We were discussing a sketch."

"Right. That's why you both jumped like two kids with their hands in the cookie jar and scrambled to hide what you were looking at. You always let me see your sketches."

"Stop interrupting me." Sophie met Mick's glare for a long moment. "Secondly, Garrett has never, ever, said or done anything inappropriate. We're friends, colleagues in our profession."

Sophie's hands were warm on Mick's cheeks. "Finally,

even if she had, I'd have immediately set her straight." Her lips brushed against Mick's. "You're the one I love, the center of my life."

Mick struggled to let go of the brooding doubts that plagued her. "Then what were you whispering about on the phone? Why did I have to go next door on some lame mission to fix the stupid hot tub?"

Sophie didn't answer. Instead, she took Mick's hand and led her through the house to the master bathroom. A soft piano concerto and the scent of honeysuckle-scented bathwater permeated the room, which was alight with dozens of candles.

Sophie turned and began to slowly unbutton Mick's shirt. "This is why I needed you to leave the house. To prepare the first part of your birthday gift."

Mick was speechless. How in the world had she gotten to this point, accusing this woman she'd trusted, loved all these years?

Sophie had changed out of the jeans and old oxford shirt of Mick's that she wore when she painted and donned a dark-blue fleece robe. Mick shrugged out of her shirt and bra and reached for the robe's tie. She slid her hands inside and pulled Sophie against her bare chest. She tasted Sophie's mint tea as she claimed those expressive lips with her mouth, her tongue.

Sophie broke their kiss and pushed Mick's pants down her hips. Her robe joined Mick's pants on the floor. "God, I love your ass."

Sophie led her to the deep tub, then lowered herself into the heated, swirling water and motioned for Mick to sit between her legs. Mick did as she bid, settling her back against Sophie's full breasts. She closed her eyes and moaned as Sophie planted tiny kisses along her neck and sucked at her pulse. A rough pinch of her nipples sent a shock of pleasure straight to her clit. Sophie knew every sensitive part of her body, every trigger that drove her arousal, as only a longtime lover could.

She slid lower in the water and lolled her head against

Sophie's shoulder. Sophie soaped her hands and smoothed them along Mick's arms, across her chest, and down her belly. Mick opened her legs to welcome the questing hands. She captured Sophie's mouth again as Sophie painted her swelling clit with the arousal pooling between her thighs—sure brushstrokes on a canvas.

Still raw from the emotion of her earlier turmoil, Mick built quickly to a climax, too quickly, and she pulled Sophie's hand away. She needed more. She needed to soothe the lingering wounds of her doubt. She burned to reassert her claim. Abruptly rising, she grabbed a thick towel.

Sophie looked startled. "Mick, what's wrong?"

"Stand up."

Confusion played across Sophie's delicate features, but she obeyed.

Mick wound the towel around Sophie and lifted her into her arms. Once in the bedroom, she gently laid her on the bed.

Sophie's knowing smile confirmed no words were needed. Opening the towel and her legs, she said, "Yours. Only yours."

Mick growled and took the offering. She lathed her tongue through Sophie's slick folds until the telltale tremble of her thighs vibrated against Mick's ears. Thankful for her lithe, limber lover, Mick pushed Sophie's knees to her chest and moved up to rub her clit against Sophie's drenched sex. Still swollen from Sophie's touch, Mick thrust slowly at first. She wanted to make this last. But her need was too great, her climax too close.

"Touch yourself," she whispered hoarsely, rolling her hips harder, faster as Sophie complied.

"That's it, sweetheart." Sophie gasped, her heels pressing into Mick's ass. "Almost there. Come with me."

Mick thrust wildly, urgently, sweat trickling down her jaw. She cried out as her orgasm swarmed through her. "Mine, Sophie. Mine."

"Yes, yes. Yours." Sophie bucked against her, and Mick

thrust her fingers inside to stroke her to a second wave of spasms.

When Mick rolled onto her back, her heart pounding, Sophie cuddled against her to trace soothing circles on her belly. Quiet while Mick's heart slowed to a normal rhythm, Sophie was the first to speak. "Are we okay?"

The tentative question tore at Mick's heart. She closed her eyes, ashamed she'd accused this beautiful woman of betraying her.

"I'm an idiot." She stroked Sophie's smooth back. "It's just…our age difference hasn't bothered me until now. For Christ's sake, my hair's completely white and you don't have a single strand of gray."

Sophie rose on her elbow to hold Mick's gaze. "I'm a redhead. So was my mother, and she was seventy-two when she found her first gray hair. You, on the other hand, were prematurely white-headed when I met you. It didn't matter then, and it doesn't matter now. I love your hair."

"Cheryl left Diane for a younger woman."

Sophie snorted. "I should have known Diane had something to do with this bout of insecurity. Age wasn't the problem between those two, and you know it."

Mick frowned. "I'm getting wrinkles."

"So am I, honey. Haven't you noticed?"

Mick studied Sophie's face. "Laugh lines. I love your laugh lines."

Tears filling her eyes, Sophie laid her hand over Mick's heart. "Do you know what scares me about our age difference?"

"What?"

"I'm terrified of the day I may have to come home to an empty house because you've left this life and me behind."

"Sophie, babe—"

"No. It's just something I have to accept, like you need to accept that I'll love you every day until then and even in death."

She wiped at her eyes and smiled. "I can't stop us from aging, honey, but I can do something about your doubts."

Sophie stood and pulled Mick to her feet. Still naked, Mick followed her into the studio to stand before a cloth-draped easel.

"When you came home early this afternoon, Garrett was going over some sketches she's been helping me with. Sketches I made to paint this for you," she said, motioning toward the easel. "It's taking longer than I thought to get it right, so instead of giving it to you for your birthday, I was going to shoot for our twenty-fifth anniversary next month." She pulled the sheet away and dropped it to the floor.

Mick stared at a handsome likeness of herself, recognizing it from a photograph taken when they'd celebrated their tenth anniversary by spending a month in the Bahamas. She'd needed a haircut, and her wind-swept locks gave her a rakish look as she stared up at the camera, her eyes a piercing blue against her dark tan.

She unconsciously pulled Sophie back against her, wrapping her in a loose embrace that mirrored the portrait. It was so lifelike, she could almost smell the cocoa butter of the sunscreen they'd worn.

"Oh, babe." Mick's throat tightened around the words. In the picture, Sophie was looking up at her rather than at the camera, her gaze so tender, so adoring it made Mick ache. "I was still young then."

"And I was thinner."

"You haven't changed at all."

Sophie turned in her arms. "I have, Mick. Look again."

Mick tore her eyes from the painting to gaze down at Sophie. "I am looking. I see the same girl in that portrait."

"And, when I look at you, I still see the handsome woman who made love to me on that beach. That's because we see each other with our hearts, not our eyes, sweetheart. I hope we always will."

Mick hugged Sophie tight against her and stared at the painting again. "You're an incredible artist."

"I am good, but I don't have much experience with portraits. Garrett helped me paint what was in my heart."

"I know I was being foolish earlier, but do we have to talk about Garrett while we're naked?"

Sophie chuckled. "No, we don't. But in the future, if something's bothering you, I want you to talk to me, not bottle it up until you start listening to Diane." Her hand feathered against Mick's cheek. "Do you have anything else on your mind I should know about?"

Mick nodded and buried her face against Sophie's neck, inhaling the sweet honeysuckle scent that lingered from their bath. "A red BMW convertible."

House of Memories

I teeter down the steps and somehow manage to shove the huge box into the moving van. What the hell does she have in here? Rocks?

"I've got to hurry or I'll miss the cable guy," she says, planting a quick kiss on my sweaty cheek. The kiss is clearly a ploy to distract me from the fact that the only thing she's carrying out of the house is her purse and two shoeboxes. "Can you walk through one more time to be sure we didn't leave anything?"

"Just make sure he gives us all the sports channels," I yell. You can't trust cable guys. The minute they leave, you usually discover they forgot to do this or that, and it takes weeks to get them to return and fix it. But she's already pulling out of the drive. I sigh and turn back to the house.

The cabinets and closets are empty. The walls are completely bare. My footsteps thud hollowly on the hardwood flooring of the living room. But as I move from room to room, I realize the house is still full...cluttered with the memories we've made here.

The hallway reminds me of the first morning I woke in her bed. It was winter and cold. She slid from our warm cocoon and threw on a T-shirt. Just a T-shirt. I watched her hurry down that hall to adjust the thermostat and nearly drooled on my pillow at the sight of her pale bottom dancing below the shirt's hem.

I realized I was heavily in lust with her.

The T-shirt was more erotic than the black teddy she'd been wearing when I'd arrived the night before. I thought that little trip down the hallway was the sexiest thing I'd ever see.

Until the study.

We'd been dating for several months and my weekends at her house were becoming a routine. I woke on Saturday morning alone in bed with the smell of coffee beckoning. I shuffled down the hall, smiling at a sudden flash of the T-shirt memory, then stopped, frozen in the doorway.

Hunched over the keyboard of her computer, she was wrapped in a short silk robe, her sleep-mussed hair sticking up in ten different directions and a pair of reading glasses perched on the end of her nose. She was adorable.

And I realized I'd fallen in love.

It was another month before I confessed it to her.

That memory was made in the living room.

We'd spent the evening lying in each other's arms on the sofa, kissing and talking and kissing while we pretended to watch a video of a Melissa Etheridge concert.

"I'm the only one," Melissa sang as our kissing evolved into slow, lazy lovemaking. She was still trembling from her orgasm as we lay heart to heart and I told her that I was the only one for her, and she for me.

Shaking myself from my thoughts, I stop in the kitchen last. I'm careful to check the places likely to be overlooked, like the little cabinet over the refrigerator and the drawer under the oven. That's when I spot it. One of her favorite refrigerator magnets has fallen to the floor unnoticed. I turn it over and chuckle.

"If you can't take the heat, then get out of the kitchen," it reads.

Resting against the sink, I stare at the empty place where the dining table had been. I pocket the magnet and pull out one last memory, closing my eyes to relive it.

❖

I've shed my shirt, walking through the house bare-chested to cool the flush of my arousal. I'm wearing my favorite baggy pair of soft faded Levi's because I need the extra room. While she's been scooping coffee, I've been making my own bedtime preparations. Did I say bedtime? With her, it can be anytime, anywhere. The thought of it makes my heart race and my nipples harden.

She's in her pajamas—soft blue to match her eyes—and busy over the sink, filling the coffeepot and setting the timer so we'll awake to its warm aroma while we're still naked, wrapped around each other, legs entwined.

I approach her from behind and press my breasts to her soft shirt. She's tall, and I have to rise on my toes slightly to kiss the back of her neck. Her scent is warm and a bit tropical, like peaches warming on the branches of a tree in a Georgia orchard. I love her smell. It's clean and feminine like her.

I wrap my arms around her and hold her hard against me. I love the way my body feels against hers. I'm all muscle and she's so soft.

"I just wanted to get this coffee ready for the morning," she tells me.

"I just want to get you ready for tonight," I purr.

"Oh, yeah? Ready for what?" I feel the smile in her voice without having to see her face.

I turn out the lights and light a few candles around the dining room, then check the back-door locks.

"I want dessert," I tell her with a smile. I hold my hand out and beckon her over, pulling her into my embrace.

Sometimes I feel the need to be slow and gentle with her. I love her and want her to know the tenderness and respect I feel for her. Other times my need is raw and hot, and that's how I feel tonight.

I'm wet and tingle around the pliant double dildo that stretches me on one end and lies warming against my belly on the other. It took some concentrated relaxation methods and a handful of lube to prepare myself this way. Its girth between my legs, bulging my jeans, adds to my swagger.

She smiles at the rap of a deep-voiced singer I've put on continuous replay. It's the first song she played for me and she'd said, "It makes me think of you."

I dance against her, turning and rubbing my back against her breasts, my ass against her crotch. She loves my narrow hips and muscled butt, and I take advantage of that whenever possible.

"Remember the night of our first date?" My voice is low and husky. "We were so hot for each other, I thought I'd throw you down on the dance floor and have you right there."

She plays along, dancing and smiling at my scene-setting.

"We could have gone into the restroom," she offers, alluding to another time when we christened the bar where we met with our ardor.

I dance around her and this time gyrate against her back, rubbing the bulge in my jeans against her buttocks and my rock-hard nipples against her shoulders. I'm so very hot for her.

Coming full circle, I take her hands in mine, urging her back until her hips are against the dining-room table.

When I push her to a reclining position, she protests. "I'm too heavy."

"No, you're not. Lie back and slide to the end," I command her softly. I've always wanted to say that to a woman. Maybe one day I'll fulfill that gynecologist fantasy.

But this comes close. She lifts her hips as I tug her pajama bottoms and panties off, exposing her as I stand between her legs and draw her closer. The rapper is chanting about going crazy with love and sex that's better than drugs.

I lick my way down her soft, white thighs, and my mouth waters as her musk reaches my nostrils. I spread her open to my eyes and my tongue. My own juices trickle around the thick dildo as I feast on her wetness.

The power I feel in taking what is mine—what she willingly gives me—is fueled by her moans. I suck hard at her clit and run my tongue along the outside of her opening. I feel her grow hot and hard, and her breath quickens. *No, not yet, my sweet.*

I take her to the edge, back off, then feast again while never allowing her release. Not yet.

I pick up another, smaller dildo I'd left on an adjacent chair and lubricate it while I continue to lick. I tease her opening with it, pushing in a little, then withdrawing. She opens to me as I slide it in and out, keeping the rhythm in time with my tongue and the rapper's croon for his lady to do what she does to him.

I feel her tense. She's too close.

Not yet, love. I'm only preparing her to be really filled.

I grab her hands and pull her to a sitting position. Smiling at the confusion I see in her eyes, I cover her mouth with my own before she can protest.

Our kiss deepens. She sucks my tongue and reaches for the zipper on my pants. She slips her hand inside, stopping for a moment when she feels my surprise. Her hand wraps around the cock and strokes so that it pushes deeper in me. I'm swollen and hot where it rubs me.

"Turn around," I tell her. It's more of a request than a command. The rapper croons that she knows how to do it, so she complies and bends over the table.

Her hips are soft in the candlelight. I love her ass. I kiss her smooth skin while spreading generous amounts of lube on the phallus that will connect my desire to hers.

I press in slowly, pulling out and pushing a little farther to allow her time to receive what I have to give. She grunts as I push in deeper and wait for her to adjust to its thickness.

I use my feet to push hers farther apart so I can lean over her back, brushing my nipples against her skin. Reaching around to tease her clit, I begin a slow thrust of my hips. I close my eyes and tremble against the urge to rush. Each stroke fills me as it fills her.

"Oh, baby." She moans.

I'm sliding in and out smoothly now, so I pick up my

speed. She begins to whimper and I signal my own impending orgasm with urgent grunts I know she'll recognize. I shift for better position and thrust hard in a fast slap, slap, slap of my hips against her buttocks.

I can't hold out as a climax swarms up from my clit and explodes in my belly, but I keep pumping and stroking her clit until she screams so loud I wonder if the neighbors are home and dialing 911.

She finally reaches behind to still my motion, and I lie heavily on her to catch my breath, to slow my pounding heart.

"I love you," I whisper.

❖

The ringing of my cell phone jerks me back to the present, and I press my hand against my throbbing crotch as I answer.

"Where are you?" she asks. "I thought you'd be here thirty minutes ago."

"Is the cable guy there?"

"Here and gone. You won't miss a minute of the big game tonight."

"Do me a favor and set the DVR to record it. I'll be there in a bit. I'm going to stop by the grocery," I say, thinking of the plump, ripe strawberries I saw there the day before. I hurry out the back door. "I've got other plans for us tonight."

I end the call and pull the door shut, realizing the memories aren't in her house, but in my heart. Tonight, in *our* house, we'll add to them.

Box of Surprises

"Sky, what are you so nervous about?" Jessica clamped a firm hand on Skyler's bouncing knee and smiled at her partner. The long leg stilled, but Skyler's gaze darted around the room like she was a long-tailed cat and all the women waiting patiently along with them were sitting in rocking chairs.

"They're all pregnant!" Skyler whispered.

Jessica chuckled. "Well, that's why they're in Dr. Nichols's office, you goof. What did you expect?"

"What if one of them squirts out a baby right here, right now?" Skyler's whisper carried, and a dark-haired woman sitting near them smiled into her magazine.

Jessica was having a hard time believing this nervous, apparently naive woman next to her was the same six-foot, androgynous blond charmer who ran a large equestrian breeding and training facility. She wasn't even pregnant yet, and Skyler was a wreck. She was beginning to think having Skyler as her demanding trainer when she'd prepared for the Olympics might have been easier than living through nine months of pregnancy with her.

"How can the sight of a pregnant woman throw you into such a panic? Is this what I've got to look forward to for nine months?"

"No." Skyler scowled and clutched Jessica's hand. "It's just…well…"

"Skyler, women, like horses, get pregnant every day. They carry babies full term, then have a normal birth—every day."

"But…"

"You've been watching the *Emergency Doctors* on the surgery channel again, haven't you?"

Skyler shrugged, an uncharacteristic blush creeping up her neck to color her cheeks and redden her ears.

"Honey, they only show the bad cases on that medical show. Every pregnancy doesn't end in an emergency. This isn't rocket science. We're just planning to have a baby."

"Okay. I know, I know. I'll chill." Skyler sighed and playfully bumped shoulders with Jessica. "We'll be fine."

"We don't have to do this, Skyler, if you're going to have a stroke over it."

"No. You know I want us to have kids. I love kids."

"I know, honey. By the third or fourth, you'll be an old hand at this," Jessica said.

"Third or fourth?"

"Kidding. I'm kidding."

Skyler blew out a breath and seemed to relax. After a moment, she grinned. "On the other hand, four would be enough to have our own polo team."

Jessica stared at Skyler. "Then you better be looking for maternity clothes in your size, too, or filling out some adoption papers."

"Ms. Black?"

They both stood and Jessica started toward the nurse. Skyler hesitated, shifting uncertainly from foot to foot. "Do you want me…uh, you know, to go with you?" she asked.

"We're in this together, all the way." Jessica pulled her along, chuckling at Skyler's wide eyes. "Buck up, stud. At least you won't be the one with your feet up in the stirrups."

❖

"So why aren't we visiting our regular GYN for this?" Skyler frowned, uncomfortable knowing her lover was naked under a thin paper sheet and that some guy would be coming in at any moment to take a peek under it. Dr. Taylor Nichols sounded like some preppy frat boy who went into gynecology so he could spend all day looking under women's paper things. She tugged at the covering, trying to tuck it tightly around Jessica's slim hips.

"Because, honey, Dr. Nichols's specialty is in-vitro fertilizations and fertility cases. Anita referred us here to give us the best chance of getting pregnant quickly."

At that moment, a knock sounded and a petite, forty-something woman hurried into the room. Jessica sat up on the table and Skyler stood protectively by her side.

"Hi, I'm Taylor Nichols." The woman smiled and extended her hand to Jessica. "And I'm guessing you're Jessica, since you're the one modeling our latest paperwear."

Then the doctor turned to Skyler and her smile became a grin.

"And you must be Skyler, the bodyguard...I mean, partner."

Jessica snorted.

"Taylor is a *woman's* name." Skyler pointedly stared at the wedding rings on Dr. Nichols's left hand and muttered, "A straight woman."

"Isn't that a stereotype, taking for granted that my wedding rings were put there by a man?" Dr. Nichols asked good-naturedly. "Although in this case, you're right."

Skyler narrowed her eyes. This woman better be straight. She was just too cute to be putting her hands in Jessica's private places...places only Skyler touched now. Jessica laughed and wrapped a reassuring arm around Skyler's waist.

"Don't mind her. She's just a little...no, a *lot*...nervous."

"Fair enough." Dr. Nichols chuckled. "Now, lie back, Jessica, and let's check things out real quick."

The exam was fast. Fifteen minutes later, Jessica was dressed and they were all sitting in Dr. Nichols's office.

"Your lab work looks good and the exam was normal. I'm glad you've already begun charting your cycle. It looks regular, which is helpful. I don't see any reason why you shouldn't be able to get pregnant."

Skyler smiled at the hope alight in Jessica's eyes.

"Now, are you planning to use a donor or a sperm bank?"

"I have a male twin," Skyler explained, "and he's agreed to donate to the cause." She was hoping, though, that the baby would have Jessica's dark hair and pale-blue eyes.

"A twin? Excellent. You two are very lucky. So, do you want to do this in the office or at home?"

"Well." She looked at Jessica for support. "My brother teaches at Princeton, but he's agreed to ship us some sticks. We'd like to try it at home. I think I know the fundamentals because I've artificially bred horses many times. It's basically the same equipment, isn't it?"

"Sticks?"

"Uh, that's what we call tubes of, uh, you know, when we breed horses. Popsicle sticks because they come frozen." She was having trouble saying the word "semen" while talking about her brother.

"Well, yes, it's basically the same procedure. Your mission is to deposit the donated sperm so that it coats the cervix at the right time during Jessica's cycle. Orgasm at the time of insemination greatly increases the chances of fertilization by helping the cervix dip into the vaginal pool and suck up the sperm. The sperm is deposited most commonly with a needless syringe. That's rather clinical, however, so one medical-equipment manufacturer has begun offering a prosthesis that allows couples to still simulate a more natural insemination if they wish. It's rather more expensive, of course."

She nodded, even though she had no idea what Dr. Nichols was talking about.

"Do you have some of the equipment you can show us?" Jessica asked politely.

Good idea. That would solve the mystery.

"We keep a few in stock, so you can take one home with you today if you want." The doctor punched a few buttons on her phone and, when the nurse answered, said, "Could you bring us one of the home kits?"

"Do you know what she's talking about?" She didn't want to be the only one in the dark.

"I think so, honey." Jessica squeezed Skyler's hand. "Just wait, and we'll see."

After the nurse delivered a plain brown shoebox-sized container, Dr. Nichols handed it to Jessica. She peeked inside, then closed it again, brushing Skyler's hand away when she reached for it.

"The instructions are there if you need any. It's pretty simple." Dr. Nichols's tone was totally clinical. "If you've handled livestock sperm, you're familiar with the basic precautions. This method is a little different because you have to remember to push the plunger slowly at the right moment. The ideal time to start pushing would be as the orgasm begins to build. This requires good communication and a sure hand. You want the entire sperm sample already deposited in the vagina when the orgasm hits its peak."

"You can handle that, can't you, stud?" Jessica teased her softly.

Images of a naked Jessica, knees up, opening herself flashed through her brain and rendered her speechless. She nodded and coughed.

"Of course, if you're unsure, we can do this in the office," Dr. Nichols offered.

Jessica tucked the box under her arm.

"No, no. I think we'll give this a try."

❖

Jessica had learned during their past year together that Skyler's body language often screamed thoughts and feelings she couldn't voice. The flush on her cheeks and her faraway look made Jessica stop at the four-star hotel just down the road from the doctor's office. She didn't even mind the wink from the butch desk clerk about their lack of luggage. She just smiled, grabbed Skyler's hand, and headed for the elevators.

When they reached the room, Jessica pulled Skyler inside and kicked the door shut. Their kisses were hot and deep. She unbuttoned Skyler's shirt, immediately found the clasp of her bra, and pulled a tight nipple between her lips.

Skyler moaned and her knees sagged. Jessica tugged at Skyler's belt buckle, then the zipper, before sliding the soft jeans and gray boy-shorts down Skyler's long, muscled legs. Her mouth watered at the scent of Skyler's arousal. She dropped to her knees and dove in without ceremony. Nothing turned her on more than this most intimate of acts.

Skyler's strangled "oh" and trembling thighs gave Jessica a sense of power that fired the heat between her own legs. She felt the pulse of Skyler's sex when she pressed her lips to it, then ran her tongue the length of her lover's clitoris to gather the growing moisture before grasping it in her teeth and sucking hard. That never failed to bring Skyler to a quick, shattering climax.

Skyler stiffened as her orgasm gripped her and let out a long groan before gently pushing Jessica away and sliding to the floor. "Holy Christ, babe. Where'd that come from?" Skyler's gaze was hungry. "Not that I'm complaining, but you still have all your clothes on and I'm naked as a jaybird."

"Then we'll just have to fix that," Jessica said, pulling Skyler to her feet and dragging her to the bed. Skyler reached for Jessica's shirt, but she grabbed her hands, stopping her. "No. You just stand there, lover. I'm in charge of this show."

She retrieved the box that she'd dropped to the floor earlier and placed it on the bed, deliberately leaving it closed. She could feel Skyler's eyes following her every move and locking on the box. Then she slowly, very slowly pulled her polo shirt over her head. She ran her fingers over her lace-covered breasts and unclasped her bra, hook by hook. She pinched and pulled her own nipples until they grew hard.

Skyler groaned when she dropped her slacks to the floor, then turned her back to bend over and slowly lower her string bikini panties. She'd learned early in their relationship that her backside was one of Skyler's prime triggers, and she used it often to torture her.

"I've been wanting to test drive one of these with you," she said, keeping her voice low and silky, as she reached for the box and handed it to Skyler.

Skyler's chest flushed red when she looked inside and lifted out a firm dildo of simulated flesh with a thong-like harness. Unlike the ones available in an adult toy store, this one had a built-in syringe to load and ejaculate semen. "Wow."

She tugged Skyler close. "I thought since we didn't have time to pick up any lube, I'd let you provide that for me." Their breasts brushed lightly, teasingly. She found Skyler's mouth with hers, tasting her lips, then asking entrance and tasting deeper as she nudged Skyler's foot to encourage her to widen her stance.

Jessica rubbed the warm, firm dildo between Skyler's legs and across her still-hard clit. Her breath hitched at the contact, but before she was too far gone, Jessica knelt and secured the harness around Skyler's slim hips. When Skyler reached for her, Jessica stepped back.

"Uh-uh, babe. You have to come to me."

When she lay back on the bed and pulled her knees up, Skyler looked as if she would either faint or orgasm at the sight. Jessica was instantly wet. She ran her fingers between her legs and held them up for Skyler to see. "This is what you do to me."

"My turn to show you what I can *really* do to you." Skyler crawled onto the bed and licked the insides of Jessica's thighs. Jessica shuddered.

"Please, Sky." She needed her. She ached for her.

Skyler moved higher and nipped at her rigid nipples, the sharp tugs distracting her until she felt the fullness of the slick cock push inside and fill her, stretch her tight. They both moaned.

Skyler was careful, gliding in and out, in and out at a slow, steady pace. Cheek against cheek, breast to breast, they coupled until the pressure was too much. Jessica's core tightened around the cock and her arms and legs around Skyler's lean frame. So good, so good. Her cry of pleasure still echoed in the room when she flipped over onto her knees and demanded, "Again."

Skyler's staccato grunts grew louder and her pace quickened. It was an erotic fantasy come to life as Jessica arched her back to meet her thrusts. Being taken like this was her deepest secret, and Jessica had never had a lover she knew would guard it and keep it safe.

"Yes," she hissed when Skyler rose to her knees, increasing and changing the angle of penetration so her clit pulled tight and swelled with each forceful stroke. "Oh, God, yes."

The sound of flesh slapping against flesh filled the room as the sensation in her belly gathered, but the strokes brought pleasure so great she almost protested the impending climax. Skyler's thrusts grew erratic and Jessica knew she must be close, too. "Oh God, baby. Come with me, Sky."

Crying out as one, they thrust together in a wild ride until Jessica finally collapsed onto the bed, exhausted. Skyler's heart pounded against her back, in perfect sync with her own. She loved the feel of Skyler on top of her, still inside her. She moaned as Skyler shifted her weight and gently pulled the cock free.

"Damn, babe. You're really good at this." Jessica rolled onto her back.

Skyler's confidence swelled at Jessica's compliment. She quickly divested herself of the equipment and flopped onto her back to pull her lover close. She loved the way Jessica's smaller body felt resting on top of hers. She ran her fingertips down the lightly muscled back and rested her hands on the firm buttocks. God, she loved Jessica's ass. She loved everything about this woman, this wonderful woman who'd given her lost and drifting soul an anchor. What had she given in return?

Skyler had only been at the bar to collect their drinks for a few minutes, but already a very attractive, dark-haired stranger was leaning close to Jessica, crowding Jessica's personal space, by the time she walked back to their table.

"You seem to be conveniently alone." The woman leaned closer than was necessary for Jessica to hear her speaking.

"My partner's at the bar, getting us a drink."

The woman reached out, grabbed Jessica's left hand, and held it up to look at it. "Must be a business partner, because I don't see a ring on this finger. Or else this woman doesn't think much of what she has."

She saw Jessica pull her hand back and frown. Time to step in.

"Here you go, love. Are you about ready to hit the dance floor?"

Jessica took the offered drink and rewarded Skyler with a quick kiss. Skyler wrapped a possessive arm around her and looked inquiringly at the other woman.

"This is my partner, Skyler Reese," Jessica said. "Sky, this is…" Jessica raised a questioning eyebrow at the woman, waiting for her answer.

The woman bowed slightly. "I can see it doesn't matter. Pardon my intrusion."

Skyler scowled as the woman retreated. The remark about the ring bothered her. She needed to do something about that.

"A penny for those heavy thoughts," Jessica said.

"Well, these thoughts are worth more than a few pennies." Skyler wiggled out from under Jessica's comfortable weight and padded across the room to retrieve her jeans. She really had planned to do this over a romantic dinner, not in the nude and in a hotel room. But the moment seemed right just the same. It was the way she wanted to give herself to Jessica, exposed and vulnerable, emotionally as well as physically.

So, Skyler knelt beside the bed, her eyes brimming with tears. After a long minute, she choked out what was in her heart.

"Jessica, will you marry me, be my partner for life?" She opened the jeweler's box to reveal a brilliant sapphire, flanked by a pair of diamonds in a warm gold setting.

When Jessica pulled back in surprise, Skyler felt a surge of panic. That reaction wasn't what she'd expected.

"I'm not asking you to change your name or anything," she blurted. "It's just, if we're going to raise children together…no, that didn't sound right…" *Damn it.* She stared down at the bed. She could never seem to say what she meant.

Jessica smiled at her.

"Oh, Sky, it's so beautiful. Yes."

"Yes?" Skyler asked hopefully.

"Yes, I'll marry you…in front of the world or in front of just a few friends. I could never love another like I love you, honey."

Skyler slid the ring onto Jessica's finger, tears finally spilling over.

"I love you, Jess. I'd be so lost without you. I want to wake up next to you every morning for the rest of my life," she said, her voice cracking with emotion. "I want to raise children with you…children who'll grow up knowing they, too, belong."

"That's exactly what I want, too," Jessica replied, gently wiping away Skyler's tears.

Skyler climbed back into bed and they held each other close, talking of the future between kisses, bonding gently, soul deep.

"You never told me you wanted to use…you know," Skyler said after a while. "I'm never going to be able to drive past this hotel again without getting horny."

"Me neither." Jessica blushed. "I wasn't sure how to bring it up. I meant to ask, did you remember to push the plunger at the right time?"

Uh-oh. "Was I supposed to do that?"

"What's the point if, when the time really comes, you forget to push the plunger?" Jessica laughed. "I think you're going to need a lot more practice, stud."

Skyler grinned. "I think I'm going to like this baby-making business."

Read Skyler and Jessica's story in D. Jackson Leigh's debut novel, Bareback.

SKIN WALKERS

Eden Thayer was a myth-buster.

She'd traveled the world, either disproving rumors or exposing the ordinary science behind a variety of so-called miracles and local legends.

After her book hit the *New York Times* bestseller list, research money rolled in at the university where she taught. The school's administration swooned at her feet. But that was three years ago, and now the pressure to produce a second book was mounting.

However, requests to investigate ghosts and pseudo-miracles were all sounding the same. She needed new material, something different, something powerful.

That's how she'd ended up on the Wyoming prairie, watching helicopter jockeys herd wild horses toward a life of captivity. The U.S. Bureau of Land Management's Wild Horse and Burro Roundup always attracted the usual animal-rights activists. The protesters were always irritating to the feds but usually harmless. Until this year.

The key to herding with helicopters was the release of a domesticated horse into the wild herd before the chase. When the wild herd hesitated at the mouth of the holding pen, this "Judas" horse would lead them inside.

At least, that's how it was supposed to happen.

This year, a mysterious black horse kept showing up and turning the herds west onto private land instead. Spooked wranglers began to babble over their evening beers about a "Jesus" horse with unnatural blue eyes. Local Shoshone whispered stories about "skin walkers."

It didn't take long for the rumors to leak out and turn the town that was the roundup's base into a three-ring circus. Television crews and tourists filled the hotels. Enterprising Shoshone donned tribal clothing and set up a camp outside of town, where they offered trinkets and ancient tales to eager tourists.

Desperate to defuse the situation, BLM agent Bill Sanders promised Eden free access and publishing rights if she could punch holes in the growing mystery so the tourists would go home and leave the feds to deal with the bothersome "Jesus" horse.

That's why she was curled in a sleeping bag on a mountain ledge overlooking a Wyoming prairie and getting ready to ride a black mustang to her next bestseller.

The beginnings of first light woke the high prairie gently, softly illuminating the flat plain of waving grass and scrubby trees. Huge mountains stood sentry at its edges, and the morning's breath carried their delicious scent of evergreen forest and water. She wasn't thirsty, but instinct told her she should drink now while nourishment was near.

She took a few steps toward the water smell and was startled at the clop of her feet against the hard ground. She looked down and froze. Hooves.

This hadn't happened since she was a child, these vivid dreamscapes in which she transformed into a horse. Not since, on the advice of a therapist, her parents sold her beloved pony, then gave away the pictures, books, and plastic models of horses that covered every surface in her bedroom. Not since they moved from their house a bike ride away from the stables to an urban neighborhood where there were no horses.

She trembled, rooted by fear that her childhood malady had returned.

But as the wind whipped through her mane and tail, her fear evaporated with the morning dew. She forgot her parents' disapproval and her therapist's cautions. She remembered only the primal joy.

She started out slow, adjusting to her unfamiliar binocular vision. Then she ran. Opening her nostrils wide and filling her great lungs, she relished the feel of her muscles sliding smoothly, her legs eating up the ground in long strides. She ran for the sheer pleasure of it, for the soul-deep elation that filled her. Her ecstatic whinny rang out and echoed back from the mountains.

The answering call brought her sliding to a halt. She stood, blowing and scenting, her breath a cloud in the chill air. Black as midnight, racing across the flat with her tail raised like a flag in the wind, the newcomer circled several times, then came to a halt in front of her.

They eyed each other. She could feel the dark mare's dominance, see it in her posture. She breached etiquette by extending her nose first, and the dark mare jerked her head to the side, her ears pulled tightly back in warning. Then she stepped forward to offer her nose, too.

They shared breath, learning of each other. Then the newcomer squealed and struck the ground with a sharp hoof, issuing an invitation as she wheeled and galloped away.

They ran, side by side, matching stride for stride as they weaved and circled in the tall grass, testing and measuring each other.

The pounding of hooves began to fade, and the *whup-whup* of helicopter blades jolted Eden from her dreamscape. She rubbed her eyes and groaned. The sun had already cleared the mountain peaks, and the day's roundup was under way.

"Damn it. Get your ass up, Thayer."

She scrambled out of her bedroll, already dressed, as the ground began to vibrate and grabbed her binoculars to focus on the approaching thunderhead of dust.

Eyes feral with fear, the wild horses fled from the sky predator that hovered low over their backs, pushing them relentlessly toward the government holding pens. She was glad now that she'd camped on a mountainside ledge, safely out of their path.

She followed the herd's flight until a foal, its young lungs and thin legs too weak to keep the pace, stumbled and fell out of the group while its panicked mother ran mindlessly on.

The baby couldn't survive on its own and the wranglers wouldn't ride out to get it, so she swung her saddle onto the rented gelding's back and hurriedly cinched the girth. He snorted and shifted nervously at the scream of a natural sky predator, and Eden spun around to witness a surreal tableau unfold.

A gigantic eagle, clutching a lifeless chicken in its talons, shadowed the helicopter that dared invade its territory, then dipped toward a new player galloping in from the west. Eden's breath caught in her chest.

"It's her."

It was clear the black horse was on a trajectory to intercept, but the herd was nearly a hundred strong, and Eden doubted it could turn them from their frantic flight. It would take something they feared more than the helicopter that dogged their heels... something big, like a..."Ho-o-ly shit!"

A grizzly bear bounded onto the plain some three hundred yards ahead of the herd and stopped. Just as the black mare joined the front-runners, the beast reared up to its full height, stretched its massive paws into the air, and roared.

The herd leaders hesitated, then followed the Black in a wide arc away from the new threat. The helicopter swung around to turn them north again, but the eagle swooped down from overhead and dropped its prey onto the main rotor, spraying blood and guts across the copter's bubbled windshield.

The mechanical bird wobbled, then abruptly turned north toward the remote airport that was its nest. The horses were safe for now...Except one.

Plaintive whinnies drew Eden back to the prairie. The

Winchester strapped next to her leg wasn't made for bear hunting, but she wasn't about to leave the defenseless baby to be an easy meal if the wind shifted and the bruin headed that way.

The little mustang stood trembling and uncertain as Eden approached slowly. Her gelding nickered to the foal, and Eden gambled on the baby's instinct to follow. Their progress would be slow with the exhausted filly trailing, so she resigned herself to another night of sleeping on the hard ground after they found the herd...if they found the herd.

❖

The herd's tracks led to a desert canyon, which led to another, then another until one appeared that was lush with grass and had a thin creek wandering through it.

The water was still muddy at its widest where the herd had obviously paused to drink, so Eden moved upstream to fill her canteen. She soaked her bandanna to wash the dust from her face while the foal drank its fill. Finished, the little filly folded its long legs and collapsed to sleep on a bed of thick grass.

"Guess this is where we'll camp," Eden said to nobody.

Her voice sounded out of place among water tinkling over rocks and wind whispering through the grass, and she ached to be something other than human in this raw and natural world.

She sighed. This was no time for dreams and fanciful thoughts.

She hobbled the gelding and set him loose to graze, then collected an armful of dead wood from under the scrubby trees that lined the creek. The moon wouldn't rise for another hour or two, so she built a small campfire, more for light than heat. Dinner was a couple of granola bars.

The filly slept deeply, and Eden fought the urge to rise and stand guard over her as a herd mate would. Instead, she pulled her bedroll around her shoulders and settled back against her saddle to sort through the swirling remnants of her day.

A series of incredible coincidences? She didn't think so. Professional animal trainers with the skill and resources to orchestrate what she'd seen today were a small group, so it shouldn't be hard to dig out the name of the rogue trainer doing this.

Eden smiled. Book number two was practically on its way to the editor.

The chapters were taking shape in her head when the gelding's rumbled greeting alerted her. A hulking shadow approached in the twilight, and an overwhelming urge to run made Eden's skin itch. Instead, she grasped the cool barrel of her rifle and slowly stood. A breeze feathered her hair back and she relaxed. Not the rank scent of grizzly.

An impatient snort broke the stillness, and the Black stepped into the ring of firelight.

Eden had seen plenty of horses with blue eyes, but they were always pintos, duns, or otherwise light-colored breeds. As far as she knew, such coloring was genetically impossible or at least rare for a completely black horse. Still, this mare's eyes were swatches torn from the summer sky.

Eden looked down. Boots. She wasn't dreaming again.

They studied each other. Nostrils flared to suck in Eden's scent, and the Black jerked her head slightly, noisily blowing out a breath as if surprised.

Eden held out her hand and the mare stepped forward to sniff it. Its eyes glowed like blue lasers, and a warm tongue washed across her palm. This animal wasn't wild, confirming her theory that a human trainer was behind this "Jesus" horse.

"Hey, beautiful. You must smell the oats from my granola bar."

The Black shook its head and stepped closer to stretch her neck in a graceful arch. Stiff whiskers tickled Eden's neck and a gentle mouth lipped at her skin. She shuddered as a flash of something familiar touched the edge of her consciousness. She cautiously brushed her fingers along satin-like hide, and the mare affectionately rubbed her broad forehead against Eden's shoulder.

Then the Black withdrew and went to the sleeping foal to nudge it awake. The little filly rose and sidled close to the newcomer, opening and closing her mouth in a submissive gesture. The Black rumbled deep in her chest as she sniffed the foal thoroughly. Then she gave Eden one last look and melted back into the darkness. A low, firm nicker summoned, and the filly lifted her head in shrill answer before hurrying to follow.

Eden listened to their fading hoof beats. She should be happy that she'd been relieved of the foal and was close to busting this myth. Instead, she felt lonelier than she'd ever been in her entire, solitary life.

❖

The tavern that doubled as a bar and restaurant was crowded, and the clatter of dishes, shouted orders, and a hundred simultaneous conversations set Eden's teeth on edge. The scent of hot sauce, greasy fries, and thick slabs of grilled meat filled the air around her, but she could still smell the stench of stale tobacco on the man who dropped into the chair across from her.

"Like I said when I phoned you, Ms. Thayer, this ridiculous rumor has gotten out of hand. The Bureau had to bring wranglers in from out of state because the locals all quit. Unemployment's over fifteen percent around here, and the salary I'm paying for a few months' work is more than most of these people make in a year when they are employed. I don't understand it."

Agent Bill Sanders waved a frazzled waitress over.

"Hey, Bill. What can I get you tonight?" the waitress asked, pulling a pencil from behind her ear and an order pad from the back pocket of her jeans.

"Cheeseburger, fries, and a light draft."

"How 'bout you, hon?"

"Just coffee," Eden said.

The waitress hurried away, and Bill returned his attention to Eden.

"Bobby says he saw you out there yesterday when that damn Jesus horse showed up and turned another herd."

"Yes, I got lucky."

"So? What do you think?"

"What I saw out there, Mr. Sanders, was a well-coordinated ambush."

"We thought it was a fluke the first time it happened, and then we cursed it as bad luck the second time. The third time, the local wranglers tucked their tails and headed back to town to get drunk and spread tales about a she-devil horse with blue eyes." Sanders glanced across the room and grimaced. "Speaking of blue-eyed devils—"

The woman striding toward them had eyes like jewels set in the sculpted angles of her long face, and her dark hair shone against her bronzed skin. A barrel-chested man with a hawkish nose and a shaggy mountain of a man trailed her, but a jerk of the woman's chin sent them to the bar to wait.

She stopped at their table, and Eden could literally feel the soft brush of the woman's curious gaze before it moved to Sanders and turned laser sharp.

"Next time your helicopters buzz my land, Mr. Sanders, I'm going to shoot their rotors off." Her voice was low and smooth, like honeyed wine, and matter-of-fact rather than angry.

"Good evening, Ms. Walker. It's good to see you, too. Allow me to introduce Eden Thayer. Eden, this is Danielle Walker. She owns fifteen hundred acres that border the federal lands."

"You should be careful of the company you keep around here, Ms. Thayer," Danielle said, her eyes still on Sanders.

He shifted nervously and scowled. "You know damn well those horses may be on your land today, but they'll return to federal land tomorrow or the next day or next week. You don't own them."

They both moved back when Danielle put her hands on the table and leaned toward him, her expression fierce.

"The federal government doesn't own them either, Mr. Sanders. They're wild, and I'll do everything in my power to see that they stay that way. The prairies belong to the wolves, the buffalo, and the wild horses. Not to the ranchers' cattle you let graze there instead. A day of judgment will come. And when nature rises up to reclaim what's hers, guns will not be needed to stop weak, selfish humans."

She was halfway across the room when Sanders, red-faced, scrambled to his feet and shouted at her back.

"You don't own the airspace, Ms. Walker, and shooting at those helicopters will only land you in a federal prison."

Danielle didn't acknowledge his threat. The hawk-nosed man scrambled after her, but the larger man cast a dark look at Sanders before he, too, followed.

"She's a nutcase," he grumbled.

Eden let out the breath she'd been holding, and Sanders waved away the plate the waitress slid onto the table.

"Just put it in a bag for me. I've lost my appetite for now."

"Sure, I can do that. But you're gonna lose more than your appetite if you try to take on Dani Walker. She's the next thing to God around here."

"She's even crazier than I thought if she believes she can tell the federal government what to do. And who's that Neanderthal that acts like her bodyguard?"

The waitress broke into a wide smile, her eyes dreamy. "Henry? He's just a big ol' teddy bear. Surely you aren't scared of him."

"Just put my food in a bag, please?"

The waitress shrugged and took the plate of food back to the kitchen.

"You can see we've got no support here among the locals," Sanders said. "I need you to crack this fast so we can arrest the people behind it. After yesterday's screwup, I received authorization to also make a sizable donation in the form of a grant to your program at the university if you can help us."

Eden should have been pleased at that news, but her mind was on the unexpected tingle that had filled her when she looked into Danielle Walker's eyes.

❖

"The name suits you."

Eden stopped her stroll down the Main Street storefronts, and Danielle Walker stepped out from a dark doorway, her eyes silver under the streetlights.

"My name?"

"It means beautiful, doesn't it?"

All traces of the intimidating woman in the restaurant were gone. Her gaze locked with Eden's, eyes begging for something Eden couldn't quite grasp. Then the moment passed and Danielle's expression dissolved into a half smile.

"You always did enjoy irony," she said.

"I beg your pardon?" Eden felt as though a conversation was going on but she still hadn't caught up with it.

"Myth-buster. Isn't that what you call yourself?"

"You've read my book, Ms. Walker?"

"It's Dani. And no, I haven't read your book. I looked you up on the Internet. Interesting work."

"It's easier than you'd think. Science or a good investigator can explain a lot that people can't or don't want to understand. In this case, I think the culprit is more likely an expert animal trainer than a shape-shifter. Surely you don't believe in people who can transform their bodies into animal forms. I'm pretty sure it'd be scientifically impossible."

Dani's eyes gleamed. "Skin-walker. Not a shape-shifter. Come with me."

Eden wasn't sure if it was a request or a command. "Why should I? I don't know you, but apparently we're not exactly working on the same team."

She was startled when Dani's hands folded around hers and warmth spread up her arms and into her chest.

"Because you need to understand the 'myth' you're trying to discredit. And because you know you can trust me."

They'd just met, but Dani touched her with the casual ease of two people who were well acquainted. Even stranger, Eden felt as if she did know her, had known her.

And she was absolutely certain she could trust her.

❖

Four Shoshone dressed in ceremonial costume sat in a semicircle around a blazing campfire. Their drumbeats, rattle-shaking, and soft chanting were a muted backdrop for a fifth man, a shaman who stood and faced the crowd of thirty or forty tourists.

He waved a bundle of sage and sweet grass over the fire, then dropped it in the flames. Even though they sat some distance away on the lowered tailgate of Dani's truck, the fire's thick smoke found them, its acrid taste bitter on the back of Eden's tongue.

The shaman's musical baritone carried easily across the open field as he alternated between song and story, laying out for mesmerized listeners the legend of Shoshone skin-walkers, warriors who were not shape-shifters but could project their minds into animal familiars.

Eden swallowed against the sharp tang of the smoke. She felt dizzy. The sound of the drums seemed to swell around her.

Listen with your heart, Eden.

It was a whisper in her ear. She glanced at Dani, but her attention appeared riveted on the storyteller. She must have imagined the words.

A sixth Indian, draped in a bearskin complete with head and paws, began to prowl the outer edges of the firelight. Eden flashed back to the grizzly she'd seen on the prairie. She thought of the shaggy-haired man she'd seen at the restaurant.

Listen and remember.

The drums were now a thousand hoof beats thundering in her ears, and a wave of nausea washed over her. She gripped the metal tailgate under her hands to ground herself. Was a branch of peyote hidden in the herbs the shaman burned?

Remember and come back to me.

She needed to get back to her hotel, away from the chanting and smoke, but she swayed when she tried to stand. "I don't feel very well," she mumbled as blackness closed in and her knees gave out.

❖

Colors swirled around her. She was tumbling, floating through a series of scenes, glimpses she couldn't hold on to long enough to make sense of them.

Terrified horses stampeded on all sides of her. She was running, too, wild with fear until a dark figure, strong and calm, shouldered through the herd to gallop beside her.

She groaned and tried to focus. Dani's face, etched with concern, hovered.

She closed her eyes and a serene plateau stretched before her. A female warrior, tall and lean in loincloth and little else, yanked an arrow from the chest of a fallen bison and turned to her. Dani's blue eyes, full of triumph, glinted above violent slashes of war paint. *Mukua dehee'ya.* Spirit horse.

Then the prairie turned to pavement, and she was riding in Dani's truck. She drifted until strong arms lifted her.

The satin sheets were cool under her fevered skin. She felt them gathering around. Murmured, worried voices. Dani's friends.

"She's fighting it. I think you should get a shaman, Dani."

"You should have gone more slowly, my friend. I know you've longed for her, but she might not be ready."

"She *is* ready. She walks without understanding, but her heart seeks mine. I know it."

Eden opened her eyes. She saw them now. Humans, yes, but more. A grizzly, an eagle, a midnight-black mare.

No, no. Impossible. The smoke. It had to be filled with hallucinogens. She gasped, and her body jerked with bone-rattling, teeth-chattering chills. Gentle fingers combed through her hair.

"Dani—"

"No. Leave us. It'll be okay."

Cold, so cold. Quick hands pulled at her clothes. A down blanket covered her, then lifted, and searing flesh pressed against her naked back. Hot, so hot.

The glare of the sun against the desert sand was blinding, so she watched the yearlings play from the cool of the tent. Warm hands slid under the light gauze of her shift to caress her breasts, and teasing lips feathered along her neck.

Johara, my jewel.

Sweet elation. *Asima, my protector. I had hoped you would find me as soon as you returned.*

Always, my sweet. But it was I who was lost until you found me.

The desert was gone and she was standing on a broad tree limb, watching a lone rider enter the forest. She grinned at the sight of the teen with startling blue eyes and ebony hair. She grabbed a vine and swung out. They tumbled together to the ground, rolling and wrestling to a stop.

Found you! Some Amazon warrior. You never saw me coming.

Ha. I let you capture me. I felt you, knew you were there. I will always know you.

The flesh under her hands was real now, and arousal coursed through her. She was hungry, starving for the body naked under hers.

She savored the tongue dancing with hers, licked at the throbbing pulse point, nipped and sucked at the hard, puckered nipples. She slid lower to nuzzle into the familiar scent and dine on the swollen flesh she had surely tasted many times before. She held tight to the narrow hips bucking under her attack. When the rock-hard thighs tensed and trembled with release, she drank of her.

At last, her fast was over.

Her heart was so full of joy that it hurt. She sobbed against the lean belly under her cheek. She rolled on her back, and Dani's long body, so soft, covered hers.

"Eden, my Eden. So beautiful. I've missed you more than words can describe."

Mouth and hands, sure and knowing, touched her in all the places that made her shudder and gasp. The sweet spot below her ear, the crest of her shoulder, the swell of her breast. Blunt nails scraped across her sensitive buttocks; teasing fingers danced along the inside of her thighs to cup her, then slide through her wetness.

"Please. I need you." She moaned. "I need you inside."

And she was filled, tight and deep. She whimpered as the fingers withdrew and filled her again. She tried to hold on to the sweet pleasure, rising to each thrust, opening to welcome the light that had been missing in her life, this lifetime. But it was too much to contain. She let go, knowing it would be hers again and again, and a burst of pleasure infused, penetrated her body soul deep.

"Dani, Dani. *Mukua dehee'ya*. My Asima." She sobbed the names like a prayer.

Dani's blue eyes glistened with her own tears now. "When we began, you were my Philippis, lover of horses." Her fingers were gentle against Eden's cheek.

"And you were my Melanippe, the black mare."

It was clear, so clear to her now.

How could she have not recognized her on the prairie? How could she have not seen it when they met in the restaurant?

"We've spent many lifetimes together, Johara, my jewel, *Nea kwee*, my wife. Each time it seems an eternity until we find each other again."

"Have you been lonely, love? It seems cruel that one of us is always born knowing and must wait for the other."

"Yes, but it makes our reunion all the more joyful."

They held each other close, stroking and gentling away the years apart, until they at last felt assured their reuniting was real.

Eden chuckled. "I guess I need to find a new occupation."

"Not necessarily. Knowing now can make it even easier to spot the pretenders. But we can talk about that later."

Dani settled onto her back and Eden curled against her side, her cheek against Dani's breast, her ear against the comforting thud of her heart. She smiled, anticipating the invitation they both knew would complete their reunion.

"Will you walk with me now?"

"Always. Forever."

They closed their eyes and found their familiars on the prairie…a black mare with sky-blue eyes and a shimmering chestnut of sun-kissed gold.

Then they were running, wild and free across the prairie, manes and tails whipping like banners. They were two hearts unfettered by time, death, or human skin.

Always. Forever.

Dance with Me

I rocked back in my chair and stared at the ceiling. The words just weren't coming easily, and every small thing—a bill unpaid on my desk, papers that needed filing, or my phone buzzing with email notifications—was distracting me.

I turned off the phone, closed my Internet browser so I couldn't see Facebook updating, and rested my fingers on the keyboard. Just start typing. Typing what? The irritating noise of the television leaked past the closed door to my writer-cave and scratched at the edges of my concentration.

The television had been an adjustment for me when Maddie and I confirmed our love and took the big step to combine our households nearly ten years ago. My dogs had grown used to her bossy cats, and we'd successfully compromised my horsey-themed furnishings with her more stylish home décor. I learned to leave my muddy boots and jacket that smelled of hay and horse sweat in the mudroom. And she packed away her collection of stuffed bears, resigned to the breeding of my Jack Russell terriers after a few became victims of their sharp teeth.

But I'd never quite gotten used to the constant sound of the television that invaded my peace when my beloved and her two cats came. The old low-definition television I rarely watched was relegated to the guest bedroom so Maddie's big-screen, high-definition unit could dwarf the living room, and her satellite dish with more than two hundred viewing choices replaced my seven-channel antenna.

I joined her on the sofa during basketball season. But once we got past that first blush of the relationship when couples can't stand to be beyond touching distance, most evenings would find me in my writer-cave and her sitting alone with her reality shows that I detested. She's okay with that, because she loves my stories of love and romance.

And I love her more than I can put into words. I savor every morning that I wake first and can wrap myself around her warm body to breathe in the light scent of the freesia-and-red-plum body lotion she uses. She invariably sighs at the contact and finds my hand to nestle it between her soft breasts so I can feel her heart thump in perfect synchrony with mine. The first flutter of her eyelashes that reveal beautiful sleepy green eyes and the murmured "Good morning, sweetie" are her daily gift to me.

Maddie is my inspiration. She is my muse.

My door vibrated once again with the bass of the television's surround sound. I smiled to myself this time and shut down my laptop. I could use some of that inspiration right now.

I found her on the sofa as expected. She was sitting Indian-style, hugging a soft throw pillow and leaning forward as her eyes intently followed the figures on the large screen. I slid onto the sofa behind her, straddling her hips and wrapping my arms around her.

"Writer's block?" she asked absently without taking her eyes from the screen.

"Uh-huh." I drew her silky blond hair back and nuzzled her warm neck. "I need some inspiration."

She didn't answer, so I sucked at her pulse and smiled when she shivered.

"What are you watching?" I slipped my hands under her shirt, but she hugged the pillow tighter to prevent me from moving upward to palm her breasts.

"*Dancing with the Stars.*"

"Put it on record and come to bed with me." I licked the side of her neck for emphasis.

"I've been waiting all week to see this, honey. I'll be furious if they eliminate my favorite soccer player instead of that stupid pro wrestler."

I gently scratched my nails along her ribs and she squirmed. "That's why we pay extra for a DVR."

"Shush. I want to hear what the judges are saying."

I huffed and released her to slump against the back of the couch. When the last judge finished his inane praise of the mediocre performance and a commercial began to air, she scowled over her shoulder at me. I was in full pout.

"Don't give me that face, Shea Whitaker. Do I interrupt when you're writing?"

"You could, if it was for sex."

She rolled her eyes but smiled and twisted around to kiss me. That was more like it. I hummed and sucked her tongue into my mouth. My fingers crept under the waistband of her flannel pajama pants, but her hand stopped their advance. The commercial had ended, so she turned back to the television. I groaned.

"Put that on hold, tiger, for just thirty more minutes," she said, tucking my wayward hand between my own legs. "Watch this with me, and then I'm all yours."

"That's a stupid show."

"I wish I could dance like that," she said wistfully, ignoring my sulk. "We met on a dance floor. Remember?"

I did remember.

It was Valentine's Day and I'd driven an hour to a lesbian bar in a different city to meet a woman I'd been chatting with online. Every relationship has a ying and a yang, and it took only one look for us to realize we were both yangs. Still, the woman was gracious and offered to introduce me around to her friends. She knew almost everyone at the bar.

After a while, she asked if I wanted to dance, mostly to

be polite, I think. Since we were both yangs, we danced an appropriate distance from each other, sending a clear signal that we were just two friends enjoying the music.

That's when I saw Maddie. She was also dancing with a friend, judging from the space between them. I watched her as she laughed at something her dance partner mouthed to her. Then, as though she could feel my eyes on her, she looked up. Her startling green eyes locked with mine, and, caught staring, I felt my face grow hot. I whirled and danced for a minute with my back to my dance partner and the enticing woman with the beautiful eyes.

When the heat in my face subsided and I turned back, Maddie had sidled up to my new friend, her mouth close to my friend's ear. My dance partner listened, and then her eyes flicked up to me. She nodded and said something in Maddie's ear.

Maddie danced back over to her friend, and my new friend grinned at me.

"What?" I mouthed the word over the loud music.

At that moment, the music changed and she motioned for me to follow her to the bar. Finally away from the throbbing music, she turned to me and grinned.

"Her name's Maddie. She wants to know if you're available."

"For her?"

"She wasn't asking for anyone else."

"No girlfriend?" How could that be possible?

"Nope. Got her heart broken about five years ago and has just been playing the field since. Go ask her to dance."

She didn't have to prompt me twice. I was already pushing my way through the crowd to request the first of many dances in those early years. It wasn't that we danced great together, because we each had our own rhythm, but we still had fun.

The last few times we'd tried to go dancing, we were stymied by head-banging metal and hip-hop tunes that had a beat neither of us could match. Ultimately, we gave up the hunt for a place that played our brand of dance music.

Now, after ten years, our animal children had grown elderly and we'd grown complacent in the romance department. Things as mundane as a writing deadline or a favorite television show now apparently took precedence over our lovemaking. But we shared the blame for that.

I rubbed Maddie's back to let her know I wasn't angry and extricated myself from the sofa. "Watch your show, babe. I'm going to give it another try." At least the characters in my book never lost their spark.

Instead of writing, though, I booted up my laptop and began searching for an anniversary gift. Valentine's Day was only a week away. I'd wanted to take Maddie on a lesbian cruise for our tenth anniversary, but she was claustrophobic, and the rooms with a view were more than I could afford.

I browsed through some jewelry websites and some vacation websites, wondering what a week in Key West would cost during the off-season. Then I saw it and my mind raced back to my earlier ruminations.

It was the perfect anniversary gift.

❖

"Really, Shea. We don't have to go out tonight." It was Valentine's Day, but it also was Wednesday—laundry and *Survivor South Pacific* night. "You're taking me to the mountains this weekend for our anniversary. That's more than enough."

"Uh, about that. I hope you don't mind, but the bookstore up there wants me to do a reading and sign books on Saturday."

She sighed. "You know I love your stories, but I thought we said no work this weekend."

She didn't need to say it. It had been years since we'd gone somewhere just for us, a vacation that wasn't a book festival or signing. Since my first novel was published the fifth year we were together, we'd spent our limited travel budget taking us to places where I could market my books and write our transportation, meals, and lodging off as a business expense.

"We'll go hiking," I said, guilt settling over me at her barely concealed disappointment. "We just have to be back in time for me to clean up and make a three p.m. reading."

She pulled on her coat and didn't speak again until we were in the car.

"So where're we going?"

The restaurant's on Martin Street. We need to be downtown for something later."

She opened her mouth, then closed it, apparently deciding to hold her tongue. I knew what she was thinking. Another book event at the LGBT Center. I could see the mixture of hurt and resentment flash across her face at this violation of our special day, and then those eyes I worshipped filled with sadness. As much as that hurt me, I let her wallow in it for now. It would make my surprise all the sweeter. At least I hoped it would.

We parked the car and I led her down the street to our destination. We paused outside the door and I took her hand in mine.

"Remember the night we met?" The small law firm where I worked as a defense attorney was right down the street. "I walk past this building almost every day and thank my lucky stars for that night."

It was a relatively new lesbian bar when we met there on Valentine's Day. It was perfect with a lounge downstairs where people could talk and play pool and a dance bar upstairs. But it didn't last long. For whatever reasons, the building had undergone several incarnations since—a health club, art gallery, then a martial-arts center.

A well-dressed couple walked up and went inside. She looked up at the three-story building. "Did they make this into a club again?"

"A restaurant. We have reservations."

There was nothing reminiscent of the former bar's black-on-white décor we remembered. Though I expected that, I was still a bit disappointed. I spoke to the hostess, who directed us past the linen-covered tables lit with candles in the muted ambience of the main restaurant.

"Surprise!" A dozen of our closest friends shouted when we walked into the room I'd reserved.

Maddie laughed. "I've had surprise birthday parties, but never a surprise anniversary."

I grinned. "I know you don't usually throw parties until the twenty-fifth, but they insisted."

We settled into our seats at mid-table and spent the next two hours enjoying our friends and some of the finest Mediterranean cuisine our city could offer. We laughed and bantered and recounted stories of camping trips, cookouts, softball games, and basketball tournaments we all had shared. But as soon as Maddie swallowed the last mouthful of her dessert, I checked my watch and stood.

"Thank you all for being here and making this a wonderful anniversary for us." I pulled Maddie up from her chair and grinned at the group. "I know some of you probably have your own Valentine's Day plans, and Maddie and I have an appointment to keep."

With that, I led her from the room amid winks and raucous comments suggesting the reason for our early departure.

❖

"That was fun, honey, and when we get home, I'm going to show you just how wonderful I think you are for arranging it." I nearly ran off the road as Maddie's breath warmed my ear and her hand crept up my thigh.

Heat rose up my neck, and blood rushed to my crotch at the throaty timbre of her voice. I intercepted her hand before it reached the intended destination and raised it to kiss her knuckles without taking my eyes from the road. "Hold that thought, babe, but we've got one more stop to make first."

I pulled into the dark parking lot of a low, single-story building with a single light illuminating the entrance. The sign on the door read Starlight Studio.

Maddie frowned. "We getting our portrait made? It looks closed."

"Nope. It's not closed." I sprang from the car and jogged around to open her door. "Close your eyes."

"Shea, I'll trip and end up sprawled in this gravel."

"No, you won't. I won't let you. Now, close your eyes and don't peek."

She wouldn't trust me with a full plate of brownies or my predictions for who would win the next NCAA tournament, but my Maddie did trust me with her safety. She closed her eyes tight, and I entwined her arm with mine to gently guide her inside.

We walked down a short hallway into a huge, open room. A disco mirror ball rotated in the center, reflecting moving pinpoints of light onto the dimly lit floor.

"Open your eyes," I said softly.

Maddie blinked. "You're taking me dancing? Alone?"

"Better than that."

The lights brightened to flood the room, and a slender, petite woman smiled as she approached.

"That was to set the mood, but we'll need more light to see during our lesson."

"Maddie, this is Selena. She's the owner and head dance instructor here at Starlight Studio."

"Lesson?" Maddie looked at me, her eyes bright with surprise.

"Shea paid for this first lesson to be private, but you'll be joining our evening class for the rest of your lessons," Selena explained.

"I'm taking dance lessons?" Maddie's gaze darted between the two of us.

"No. We're taking dance lessons. Together."

"We have several gay and lesbian couples in our class," Selena said.

Maddie shrieked and jumped into my arms, wrapping her legs around my waist. She would have knocked me down if I hadn't been two inches taller and more sturdily built. She peppered my face with kisses and Selena laughed.

"We'll start with a waltz, then go through some basic salsa steps to catch you up with the class. I'm hoping I can also convince you two to try my favorite later. You're perfectly paired for the tango," she said, indicating our fairly trim physiques and close match in height.

Maddie dropped her legs to stand on her own again but pulled me down for a deep kiss. When she released me, I glanced at Selena, wondering if my ears were as red as they felt. But she'd discreetly turned her attention to the music CDs on a nearby table to give us a moment of privacy, so I gazed down at Maddie. Christ, she was even more beautiful than the day we met.

She touched her forehead to mine. "Thank you for this. It's the best gift ever."

"I wanted something we could share." I stopped to swallow past the lump that formed in my throat. "The class is at the same time as *Dancing with the Stars*," I said, foolishly insecure that she might choose the television over spending time with me.

She threw her head back laughed gleefully. "That's why we pay extra for a DVR." She stepped back and tugged me toward Selena. "I'd rather be dancing with you."

Maddie stopped and raised an eyebrow at the relief that must have shown on my face. "And after our lesson, stud, you're getting so lucky."

Now, it was my turn to laugh and, again, thank my lucky, dancing stars.

RIDING PASSION

Luna

"Are you asleep?" I spoke softly so that I wouldn't wake her if she were.

Haze rolled over and stretched languidly before raising the head of her lounger from flat to reclining. Nearly naked, she was an androgynous delicacy that watered my mouth and heated my belly with every sweep of my gaze, every stroke of my charcoal pencil.

The plump bead of perspiration that trailed down her neck, over her sculpted collarbone, and between her small, high breasts made my throat convulse with the impulse to lick it from her body. Diverted by the contour of her ribs, it dripped down to the thick towel under her. Opportunity lost.

She blinked lazily at me. I *had* awakened her. Actually, she'd awakened me. The compulsion to map her image on paper was my futile attempt to decipher what caused me to desire her with every breath.

"Luna." My name rolled off her tongue like a caress. "Haven't you captured me sufficiently already?"

I answered with a slight shake of my head, but pondered the double meaning of her words as I flipped to a fresh page and began to sketch her new position.

Her black, low-riding boy shorts were a modern loincloth on her long, lean body. Haze loathed the men's underwear that some lesbians preferred. I loved that about her. She was a wonderful mixture of masculine and feminine, strength and sensitivity, toned muscles and downy skin.

I sketched her masterful—sometimes I thought magical—long-fingered hands that rested on the towel alongside the narrow hips that fit so perfectly between my thighs. I shivered in the heat, and the small smile that teased her lips told me she'd noticed.

Haze craved the bright, burning sun, and it had lightly bronzed her creamy Celtic skin and darkened her nipples in recent weeks. I, on the other hand, sheltered my olive skin with long sleeves and a wide-brimmed hat.

I found *my* center in the shadows of the moon. I was night and she was day. I circled; she was direct. I teased and she stalked. I was cautious, using my drawings as a thin shield to refract her power. She was fearless, laying herself bare to me in lustful, longing poetic verse.

Opposites attracting? No. Completing. Two arcs making a sacred circle. Sunset, moonrise, dawn, then dusk. Two celestial bodies in a continuous, symmetrical dance.

The codependency startled me, and a sudden malaise squeezed my chest.

The moon wielded her *own* power. Danced to her *own* music. Flirted with whatever stars came out to play. Teased the night with her constant changes—quarter, half, full, blood, blue, harvest. She didn't need the sun.

I sighed. But without the sun and its light, there would be no dark, no night, and no moon.

I threw down my sketchpad. "I'm going into town for a bit," I said.

Haze sat up, instantly alert. "Give me ten minutes to shower and dress."

"No need, I'll be back in a few hours." But I did need her… every second, every minute, every hour of the day. I didn't want to leave her, even for a few hours, but I needed to prove that I could.

I turned away before I could bite back my words and soothe the look of confusion from her handsome brow. Her vulnerability was an effective weapon.

I stood in the cool dark just inside the double doors that opened to my bedroom and tossed my hat onto the low chaise. Haze followed and pressed her sun-heated flesh against my back. The aroma of cocoa butter and sweat and sunlight filled my senses. When her arms closed around me, my resolve wavered.

"What is it?" Her arms tightened and her mouth pressed to my ear. "Luna? You're trembling."

"You're a distraction, Haze." I frowned, turning and pushing against her chest with my hands. "And I don't know what to do with you."

"Then we're even. With you, I don't know if I'm going or coming."

I realized I had dropped my hands to her breasts, and her nipples were firm knots against my palms. This was insane. Of course I knew what to do with her. Every cell in my body screamed it. I whirled us around and backed Haze toward the bed. "Coming," I said. "You're definitely coming."

We'd made love a hundred times over the past weeks, and each time, her passion claimed another tiny piece of my heart. But this time would be about sex. I would deny her power. I would take her and give away nothing. I would sate myself and walk away, if only for a few hours.

She fell back against the bed, the surprise skittering across her features turning to consent when I yanked the boy shorts down her hips. I stared at her for a long moment, letting her see my desire that prowled like a great hungry tiger. Then I pounced.

I pushed her thighs apart as I licked the salt and buttery oil from her belly, from the juncture of her hips, from the inside of her legs.

"Luna." She squeezed her thighs inward. "Come up here and flip around so I can have you, too." Her fingers tangled in my hair, but I grabbed her wrists to pull them free and corral her hands against the bed.

"No." I wouldn't let her love me. "Open your legs." I bit her quad, hard enough to make her jerk open to me again. Full and flushed and glistening, she made my mouth fill and my jaw clench as I breathed her in. I kissed my teeth marks in a small apology and held tight to her wrists as I explored her with my tongue. The more she writhed, the more care I took not to linger in the spot that hitched her breath, bucked her hips.

"Baby, please."

The edge in her plea bordered on pain, so I scraped my teeth against her pulsing flesh, then sucked her into my mouth. I released her hands and held on when her hips rose with her strangled cry. Her body bowed and held for a long minute, and, when she collapsed again, I stood and stripped off my clothes.

Her skin was slick from oil and arousal and exertion, so my body slid easily along hers. My nipples firmed as they scraped over the ridge of her ribs and met her breasts in a rough kiss. Her heart still thundered against my chest, her eyes still unfocused from her climax. I mounted her, straddling her hips. She roused and tried to leverage her hand between us, but I denied her. She was lean, and the thin flesh that covered her pelvic bone would bruise under my forceful thrusting, but I didn't relent.

I dropped my head back and closed my eyes to focus on the pleasure I'd take from her. That's what I did with women. I took my pleasure from them and moved on, my freedom, my independence intact. I am Luna. I did not need the sun.

"God, you're so incredibly beautiful." Her words were fierce, gritted out as her jaw clenched against my abuse, but her eyes were bright as she pressed upward to give me what I sought. Haze twisted her wrist from my grasp and entwined her fingers with mine instead. "Ride me, baby. Ride me hard. Come for me. You can do it."

When her free hand found my breast and twisted my nipple,

I lost it. I found it. I dropped my head back again and screamed at the ceiling. When my orgasm drained from me, I collapsed, limp and sweating on top of her. She gentled me with soft strokes along my back and reverent kisses along my face.

I had run for the gate only to discover I had been the fence containing me. She was not imprisoning me. Haze was dragging me to freedom. I'd found victory in surrender. I was in love with her. Strangely enough, it felt like strength rather than weakness.

Still, being a cautious person, I couldn't reveal this fact to her, confess her hold on me until I was confident it wasn't just the rush of endorphins. I was sure, however, that I could no longer put off what I'd been dreading.

"I have to leave in the morning to attend a gallery opening of a close friend."

Her hands stilled their stroking and her silence was a vast chasm. "I can go with you if you like," she said at last.

I could hear her uncertainty. It would be her first venture back into the public eye after a firestorm created by the rumor that she and our president's wife were having an affair. My heart swelled at her offer because I knew that while she shared herself as Haze Baird, the renowned poet, Haze the woman was very private. She was an old soul, often formal in her manner and verse, yet with a childlike, vulnerable heart. The affair manufactured by the president's political enemies had cut her open, wounded her in a way that wasn't quite healed. I could not, would not make her bleed again. Not for my sake.

I stared into her forest-green eyes and stroked her cheek. "It's in Washington, blocks from the White House," I said gently. "If you go with me, I'm afraid the media will focus on you rather than my friend's gallery opening."

Emotions, too many and too fleeting to identify, raced across her features. "How long will you be gone?"

This was where I should soothe her with words of reassurance. And what could be more binding than to confess I'd fallen for her? But she, who writes lovely, lustful poetic tributes to my allure, hadn't yet admitted love either. My insecurity held me back.

"I'm not sure. While I'm on that side of the country, I need to visit the galleries in New York and Philadelphia that carry my paintings." I kissed her softly. "Besides, you should be able to write reams of poems without me to distract you. You said you need maybe a dozen more to complete your next book."

She sighed. "You don't distract me. You inspire me."

I kissed her again, my lips brushing, my tongue exploring. How would I survive even a day, much less weeks, without her mouth? I pressed my cheek to hers for long seconds, breathing in her scent, savoring the press of her small breasts against mine. If I lingered much longer, we'd never get out of the bed. But I had things to do, and I wanted to get them out of the way so the evening, the night would be for us. "Let's shower and go to town so I can take care of some business. Then we'll do whatever you want this evening," I said, reluctantly abandoning her warmth.

Haze stood and drew me to her. "I want to go for a ride on the beach under the moonlight."

I smiled. "Yes. I want that, too."

❖

"You can ship these four to the new gallery in D.C." I loved to paint but had little patience for the business of being an artist. Angelo owned the local gallery, but I also paid him to handle requests and ship my work to other galleries. My lawyer, Susan, took care of my gallery contracts. The only thing I managed personally was the money.

Haze's boots were loud on the stairs leading up to the gallery's loft. She carefully deposited three more canvases against the wall. "That's the last. I'll wait for you downstairs," she said.

Angelo spread the stack of paintings out to peruse them. "Amazing," he muttered. He studied me as he had each painting.

"These are definitely your best." He glanced at Haze's retreat and raised an eyebrow at me. "You've been incredibly inspired and productive these past weeks."

I ignored his insinuation, refusing to throw fuel on his embers of gossip. "I got a call from a gallery in Chicago. The owner saw my work in the New York gallery and would like some of my paintings." I pointed to two of the ten I'd brought and handed him a slip of paper. "You can send those to this address when Susan emails that she's received a signed contract from them."

"That's going to leave you short in filling the requests from New York and Philadelphia."

"How many do you have in your inventory?"

He hummed as he counted in his head. "Six, I think."

"Then let's go downstairs and pick two from them. I'll be back in plenty of time to paint some new ones for you before the tourist season starts again."

Angelo nodded and I followed him carefully down the steep stairs. We'd only descended halfway when he stopped so suddenly, I had to grasp his shoulder to keep from falling over him. "You've got trouble," he said.

His warning held an undercurrent of glee that made me want to roll my eyes. He might get fresh gossip after all. Haze stood at the back of the gallery with Jackie.

"What's she doing here?"

"I think she's stalking you," he stage-whispered. Angelo loved to manufacture situations, especially when they involved my social life, which he claimed was better than a reality show.

"What makes you think that? I haven't even spoken to her in months."

Angelo dramatically stared up at the ceiling and ticked off the reasons on his fingers. "One, she's rented the apartment above the bakery across the street and sits on the balcony every day, watching for you. Two, she comes in here almost daily to stare at your painting of her. Three, she tried to pry information from me about your latest." He nodded toward Haze.

"Haze? What did you tell her?"

"Nothing, but she's seen you two in the market and managed to put things together. Only a few months ago, your friend was the subject of a media feeding frenzy. Hard to miss."

They were standing in front of my display of paintings, their voices low enough that I couldn't distinguish their words. Haze's expression was unreadable. What must Jackie be saying to her? I approached cautiously, Angelo close on my heels so he didn't miss anything.

"Hello, Jackie." I resisted my urge to wrap a protective arm around Haze. If Angelo was correct, I didn't want to antagonize Jackie. I didn't want to engage her either, so I surveyed the paintings on the wall and pointed to a seascape. "That one," I said to Angelo. My eyes settled on the one of Jackie, lounging nude in a window seat as a burning cigarette dangled in her fingers. If it was gone, maybe she would go, too. I pointed to it. "And that one. It should sell easily in New York."

"No!" Jackie jumped forward and took it from the wall. "I want to buy it."

Her desperation was embarrassing, and I was ashamed that our interlude seemed to have reduced the cocky woman I'd known to this frantic one. I was acutely aware of Haze watching me.

"If you want it, it's yours," I said. "A gift."

She scowled. "I don't want charity." She turned to Angelo. "How much?"

Jackie wasn't poor, but not rich either. I knew the price I could ask in New York would be more than she could spare, and I apparently had already stolen her dignity. I wouldn't take more from her.

I held up my hand to forestall Angelo's reply. "Five hundred for Angelo's commission." I searched for a way to make her take the painting and accept that our moment was gone. "If you won't accept it as a gift, then consider it payment for posing for me." I cringed as soon as the statement left my mouth. I was terrible at choosing words. I should have instead drawn a picture for her—me waving good-bye, a door closing, the sun going down on our tryst.

She glared at me, her throat working. "Then I was just a high-priced whore to you?"

"No. You were a friend, but you wanted more and I didn't, I don't." I held her gaze. "Please take the painting, Jackie. A memento, not a payment." I pointed out a different painting to Angelo. "Send that one to New York."

"The seascape to Philadelphia then?"

"Yes." I was relieved to disengage from the tête-à-tête with Jackie.

He gently took the painting from her. "Should I wrap this for you?"

She gave Haze a long, resigned look before she answered. "Can you box it? I'm packing up and heading back to San Francisco in a few days." I heard decision, not rancor in her voice, and she followed Angelo without sparing me a glance or a good-bye.

I looked at Haze and was surprised to see irritation burning in her eyes as she watched Jackie retreat. "I'm done here. Are you ready to leave?" I asked.

"More than ready," she said, taking my hand to lead me out. "Let's have dinner in town, at that tapas place you like."

"That sounds wonderful," I said, relieved that this awkward meeting hadn't derailed our day.

❖

"What's this?" I'd intended to ride Zephyr, my stallion, but my stable manager, Juan Carlos, was leading one of my favorite mares, Passion, from her stall.

"Ah. It's good that you're here. I can use some experienced

help," Juan Carlos said. "She's come into season sooner than we expected," he said. "It's time. I can hold her while you handle the stallion."

Haze frowned. "You don't artificially inseminate?"

Juan Carlos raised his eyes toward the roof in a silent supplication. I smiled at the gesture, wondering if his plea to the heavens was for the short version of my usual lecture or for Haze to be the one to change my mind on this issue. Since even his deity couldn't change my opinion about breeding naturally, I conceded by keeping my reply brief.

"How would you like it if you were feeling amorous, and instead of satisfying your need, I stuck a plastic tube into your vagina?"

Haze glanced at Juan Carlos and flushed a deep red. Juan Carlos made an impatient noise at my blunt language but said nothing. I expected that from him. I didn't expect the words Haze whispered for only me to hear.

"Depends on the thickness of the tube. The right girth can provide as much pleasure."

My face heated as I envisioned a different kind of moonlight ride. "You might have to prove that to me later," I murmured.

Her lips brushed against my neck in promise.

I slid open the door to Zephyr's stall, and he eagerly gave me his head to halter. He was very well mannered for a stallion but couldn't contain his enthusiasm and called out his desire with a neigh that bounced off the barn walls and rang in our ears. We laughed as we stepped out into the waning sunlight and followed Juan Carlos to the paddock, where he loosed Passion and held the gate for Zephyr to follow.

"You should at least muzzle her. We had to stitch up one of her love bites last time." Like most men, Juan Carlos felt only females should bear the pain of procreating. I blamed his Catholic upbringing.

"Pain is the price of love," I said. I knew this too well. My heart already ached in anticipation of the coming weeks of separation, and I was calculating whether I could forgo the New York and Philadelphia gallery visits to return sooner. I leaned into Haze, and she wrapped her arm around my shoulders as we watched the two horses circle each other, then run the paddock together.

They were a magnificent pair, high stepping, manes and tails flying in the wind. At last, Passion stilled in the center of the paddock, raising her tail and expelling spurts of pheromone-laden urine. A horsey come-fuck-me invitation. Zephyr approached and, after a perfunctory sniff, rose to mount her. She stepped forward and unleashed a kick that barely missed his leg.

Juan Carlos swore under his breath.

Haze barked a laugh. "She's playing hard to get."

I shook my head. "She wants more than to couple. She's demanding his passion. How do you think she got her name?"

The stallion circled and the mare stilled again. He took his time, inhaling her pheromones and nipping at her rump. She widened her stance and raised her tail again. He nipped her hard and extended an impressive penis. She squealed a sharp whinny and stamped her front foot impatiently. He mounted quickly and grunted as he thrust into her. In less than a minute, he dropped back to the ground. It was done.

Juan Carlos clipped a lead to the stallion's halter and led him to the gate. "Sorry if this spoils your plans for the evening." He was well familiar with my preference to ride in the cool of the night.

"We'll still ride."

Watching the breeding with Haze left me wet and urgent. I wanted her between my legs. I also wanted to prolong the sweet torture of anticipation.

"Shall I saddle Zephyr for you then?"

My answer was for Juan Carlos, but the words, the heat in my gaze were all for Haze. "No. I feel like riding Passion tonight."

❖

Twilight was giving way to moonrise when we emerged from our tunnel onto the beach, and I urged Passion immediately into a brisk canter. I needed the wind on my face, the sting of salt against my skin, and the sound of Rika's pursuit in my ears. I would dream of it on those lonely nights when I would long for Haze.

We came upon a huge piece of driftwood lodged against an outcrop of boulders, and an impulse seized me. I reined Passion to a stop and dismounted, tying her to the wood.

"What are you doing?" Haze dismounted to join me.

"I want to swim," I said, shedding my clothes and laying them on the boulder. "Come with me."

She grinned but sat to pull off her boots. "You're crazy, you know."

Haze did make me giddy, but I wasn't crazy. I laughed. "I'm passionate," I said.

Naked, we joined hands and ran into the warm surf. It knocked us down a few times, but we held tight until we were past the breakers and Haze drew me to her. Her lips and mouth tasted of the sea. Her body was lithe and strong against mine. I wanted to drown in her.

I could wait no longer to have her, to let her have me. Buoyed by the water, I wrapped my legs around her waist. Her hand curled under my leg and her fingers found me. I plunged my tongue into her mouth and she filled me with her fingers. The ocean rocked with us, pulsed around us. My orgasm hit hard and fast, and I raised my eyes to the stars with a gasp when it gripped me. She was my blazing sun and her light infused me, shone through me.

Spent for now, I bowed my head to rest on her shoulder, and we listened to the relentless lap of the waves. Silently, I lowered my legs and took her hand, the one that had been inside me, and led her to shore.

The rocks still held the sun's heat, and we climbed onto a

large flat one. She shivered in the warm air when I began licking the droplets of ocean from her neck, her breasts, and down her belly. I wanted a taste of her to take with me. She pulled her knees up, giving herself to me. I was so hungry for her and she so ready for me. She groaned out her climax long before I had my fill. I would never have my fill of her.

We turned to each other in surprise when male voices sounded down the beach. We scrambled to dress as they grew closer, then mounted quickly and rode laughing in the opposite direction, toward the hacienda.

Juan Carlos had waited for us, taking the horses and saying nothing about our wet hair and disheveled clothing.

"Shower," I said. "Come shower with me."

We teased and soaped each other until we were frenzied again.

"Bed. Now." The edge in her demand told me she wouldn't wait, and I detested climbing into bed with wet hair, so I held her against the tiles of the shower wall and parted her thighs with mine.

"Not yet," I said. I kissed her hard, gripped her and squeezed. She was hot and hard for me. I thrust up into her, the heel of my hand massaging her turgid clit. It was good that my hands were strong from long hours of holding pencil and brush, because she liked to be handled a bit rough.

"Yeah, babe. Just like that." Haze braced her hands on my shoulders when I moved down to take her nipple in my teeth. I bit hard and she tightened around my fingers.

"Fuck, fuck." Her strangled cry was my trumpet of victory.

She slouched against the tiles, her eyes gleaming. "That buys you five minutes to dry your hair."

I laughed. The fact that she knew me enough to see through my tactics warmed me in new places, deep places.

She toweled off quickly and disappeared into the bedroom. I was jealous that her hair was coarser and dried quickly, while mine was like fine strands of silk that held the water. She watched impatiently while I worked the hair dryer, but groaned and disappeared into the bedroom when I bent over to dry the underside. I realized my position and smiled at the unintended tease.

I switched off the bathroom light and realized the bedroom was already dark. Haze had opened the double doors to the portico, and my eyes adjusted quickly to the moonlight that rode the ocean breeze. Where was she? I went to the doors, but the portico was empty. Then I felt her against my back.

I turned in her arms, her eyes green jewels as she watched me. Her hips met mine. Something was different. I dropped my gaze slowly to her chest, to her belly, to her hips and what was strapped to them. She whirled us around and walked me backward to the bed. Had it only been this afternoon that I had done the same to her? Not the same. This was different and my blood simmered with it.

Haze lowered me to the bed, keeping her legs between mine. She held my gaze as she picked up a small bottle of oil, but my attention was drawn to her hands as she thoroughly coated the length of her appendage. Incredibly sexy, but unnecessary. I slickened, nearly dripped with each stroke of her hand.

Wordlessly, she grasped my legs and bent them upward as she crawled onto the bed. I sucked in a breath as she stroked my swollen flesh, then pushed inside. She smiled at the easy glide. "Are you ready for me?" Her husky voice was the dark velvet of night beckoning my moon.

"Yes," I breathed. "Please."

Haze filled me boldly in one stroke and held. The pleasure was so great, I dug my heels into her thighs. "Yes." I moved against her. I had to feel it again and again. I would beg now and always for this, for her, for her passion.

She stroked slowly and I writhed with the sweet torture. Her slow pace kept me on the precipice. I wanted to stay there forever, yet I wanted to leap over. I wanted. I needed. Moans filled my ears. My moans. It was more of a roll than a leap. Still I screamed when the dam burst and my belly clenched so hard my shoulders rose from the bed.

Still, she stroked. Harder now but no faster.

"So good," I moaned and cupped her face as she hovered over me. "So good."

Her mouth found mine, her lips and tongue possessive. We panted when she broke off her kiss, and I protested when she withdrew from me. But she ignored it and pulled a pillow next to my hips.

"I'm far from done with you," she said. "Roll over."

She tucked the pillow under me so that it raised my hips, and she filled me again. "Oh, Haze. Yes. Like that. Yes. Oh, fuck. What are you doing to me?" Her cock had found a spot inside, a treasure I'd never experienced. Her sweet weight pinned me, her rigid nipples raked against my shoulders, and her breath was hot in my ear. "Don't stop, don't stop." I wanted it to never end. I wanted to forever feel the jerk of her hips against mine, hear the slap of her flesh against my ass.

Her pants were grunts now and my moans sharp whimpers. Harder, faster. We reached for the peak together and flung ourselves over. The French call it *la petite mort*. The small death. And I wished to die with her again and again.

❖

Haze still slept when I rose early to shower and dress. I took my gift from its hiding place in the guestroom closet and propped it against the chaise, where she was sure to see it.

I longed to kiss her, to see those sleepy emeralds looking up at me. But if I touched her, I would want more. It would be too difficult to go, and Juan Carlos was waiting to drive me to the airport an hour away.

So I scribbled a note. I wasn't brave enough to say it all, but I hoped what I'd written would tell her how deeply I need her.

I knew if I woke you I wouldn't be strong enough to leave, so I'll let last night's kisses be our good-bye.

Reindeer Roundup

Tory cursed when still another string of red and green lights blinked off. She flung the garland in her hand to the floor and turned to get the box of replacement bulbs from the coffee table, groaning at the sound of glass ornaments crunching under her foot.

"I give up," she shouted to the empty room. She flopped down onto the couch and stared out the window at the eight inches of fresh snow.

What the hell was she thinking when she let Leah talk her into buying all these decorations? Oh, yeah. She was thinking they'd be sipping warm spiced wine and stringing lights together to celebrate their first Christmas.

Four months had passed since she and Leah had admitted their love for each other and openly began their courtship. Three of those months had been the most exhilarating of Tory's life.

They'd taken a day-long horseback ride in the Appalachian Mountains when the leaves changed to an autumn palette of red, gold, and brilliant yellow. They'd shared afternoon picnics and candlelit dinners, art exhibits, and shopping trips. For one cozy week, they'd hidden out at a private cabin and skied the slopes at a nearby resort.

What she'd loved the most, though, were the simple moments when they cuddled on her couch to watch a DVD or laughed together at the antics of their overly curious Chincoteague foal, Sure Thing.

Those nights when they opened their hearts and shed their clothes to explore their passion in every soft curve, every sensitive pulse of each other's bodies were wonderful beyond description.

Not much about them was similar. Leah was a petite brunette, while she was tall, athletic, and blond. Leah was an outspoken steel magnolia, whereas everyone described her as laid-back. As a journalist, Leah took things apart to expose what was wrong. As a veterinarian, she put things back together and made them right again.

Despite their differences, like two polar ends of a magnet, they were drawn together by a force too powerful to resist. That's why the past few weeks, when work had pulled them in different directions, had been pure torture. Leah had recently won a new contract to help shape a new legislative proposal on extended home care and was busy lining up witnesses to testify before the Virginia General Assembly in January. Tory was glad that Leah's new venture—consulting work based out of Cherokee Falls— was already paying off. But damn it, it was hard to be apart so early in their relationship.

Leah had first said she'd be away only a week, and they'd talked on the phone several times a day. When the work took longer than expected, Tory had driven to Richmond for a promised two days of making love and ordering room service in a fancy hotel suite. The weekend of passion had melted away on Saturday morning with the fifth phone call for more information. Tory ended up watching television alone while Leah spent most of the weekend working at her laptop with an apologetic, but very attractive and openly lesbian lawyer.

Tory had returned to Cherokee Falls on Sunday night, clutching to her heart Leah's vow to be back home before the next weekend. But by the end of the second week, Leah's phone calls had become less frequent, and when they did talk, Leah was too tired to carry on much of a conversation. On Thursday, she'd called to say they still hadn't finished. To make it home in time for Christmas, she'd have to work through the weekend again and most of the next week.

So, here it was Sunday afternoon and no Leah. Tory surveyed her halfhearted attempt to decorate the tree alone, her heart growing heavier with each wink of the cheerful lights. Their last conversation on Friday kept replaying in her mind, awakening every devil that had ever plagued her.

We're working every minute of the day, honey, Leah told her on Friday night, but she sounded distracted, and Tory could hear giggling in the background. She'd hung up without the soft sighs and confessions of love and loneliness that usually concluded their phone calls. The real knife in her gut, the ache in her chest, came from the fact that Leah hadn't seemed to notice.

Her depression was a heavy weight. Lugging it around the past two days had exhausted her. Tory leaned her head back and closed her eyes. She imagined Leah calling to say her work in Richmond had reminded her why she liked living in large cities. She imagined Leah saying things just weren't going to work out for her to live in Cherokee Falls.

Those thoughts were her last until cold hands and warm lips feathered across her face and drew her from a troubled doze. She blinked several times to focus on eyes the color of dark honey and realized the weight pinning her legs was Leah straddling her lap.

"There they are," Leah said softly. "I've been missing my leprechaun's green eyes."

"You didn't call me yesterday," Tory said, her voice gruff. *How much have you really missed me?*

"You hung up Friday without telling me that you love me," Leah said, her words more of a question than an accusation.

Tory didn't answer and averted her eyes, ashamed for Leah to see the mistrust in them.

"You hung up before I could tell you how much I was missing you," Leah said, stroking Tory's cheek.

"You sounded busy…and distracted. You sounded like you weren't alone." Tory scowled, still refusing to meet Leah's gaze. "I could hear someone laughing."

"Ah. I see." Leah shrugged. "You caught me. I met another woman in Richmond. She's very cute and blond like you. But her eyes are blue. The prettiest color blue I think I've ever seen. I fell in love with her the first time I met her."

"I don't want to hear about it." She couldn't believe Leah could be so casual about another woman. She couldn't look at her and didn't want to be touching her. Tory tried to push her away.

But Leah locked her hands behind Tory's neck and hung on tight. "And she's ten years old."

Tory stopped her struggle. She blinked back tears and looked up at Leah. "Wha…what?"

"That was Alisha's ten-year-old daughter. We were working at their house because her partner had to attend a fund-raiser and they couldn't find a sitter."

Relief and embarrassment flooded Tory. She buried her face in Leah's neck. She felt like a big baby, a big jealous baby.

"Oh, sugar. This is my fault." Leah tightened her arms around Tory. "I know there were times when we first met that I pushed you away. But that was before I gave you my heart, darlin'. Don't you know you own me?" Leah stroked Tory's back. "I've always been able to lose myself in work. But when you didn't call me at all yesterday, I told Alisha I had to go home. If the snow plows had cleared the roads sooner, I would have been here last night."

"Really?"

Leah chuckled at Tory's muffled voice against her neck. "Really, sugar."

"I was afraid you'd changed your mind about us. That maybe you decided Cherokee Falls was too small and dull for you."

"No, baby, never. Christ almighty. I missed you so much I

actually had a wet dream about you. It was so real I woke up in the middle of a huge orgasm."

"You dreamed about me?" Her dark cloud lifting, Tory pulled Leah closer.

"Night and day." Leah slipped her hands under Tory's shirt and raked her nails along her spine. "Now, what are you going to do about making those dreams come true?"

Tory nuzzled Leah's neck. "You smell like chocolate."

Leah leaned back and lifted her chin to expose a tiny reindeer tattoo on the pulse point just below her jawline. "Compliments of my young girlfriend. Taste it."

Tory sniffed at the reindeer, then tentatively stroked it with her tongue. "Mmm. Chocolate mint." She couldn't resist planting kisses along the length of Leah's neck. "My favorite flavor on my favorite person. I love early Christmas gifts."

"Oh, no, sugar. This gift is for me." She hummed with pleasure when Tory's mouth found the tattoo again, then gasped as Tory sucked hard. Leah rubbed her crotch against Tory's stomach. "I've got Santa's whole team hidden all over my body. It's your job, lover, to find every one of those little fellers and lick it off before you get me so hot they melt."

Tory growled, her mouth never leaving Leah's neck as she stood and wrapped her arms under Leah's hips to carry her to the bedroom. No one but Leah had ever provoked such an aggressive need to possess and protect.

Dasher was nothing but a lingering bruise on Leah's neck, and when Tory spied another nestled in Leah's cleavage, buttons flew across the room. A scrape of her teeth, a lashing of the tongue, and Dancer was a casualty, too.

Leah's body was her battlefield, and each tiny reindeer devoured was another doubt conquered. Leah belonged to her. No job, no other woman was going to steal her away.

It took some effort, but she slowed her attack when she discovered Prancer covering a puckered nipple. Torture by tongue was to be his sentence for hiding in such a coveted place.

"God, I've missed your mouth on me." Leah moaned as Tory freed her breast of the invader.

She found Cupid prancing low across Leah's soft, lean belly, his antlers poised to guard what Tory came to claim. She attacked swiftly, wielding her tongue with deadly accuracy and moving on.

Vixen was patrolling the inside of a firm thigh, and Tory pushed Leah's knees apart to pounce. The sweet mint that coated her lips mingled with the heady scent of Leah's arousal. She nuzzled into that wet heat, painting her lips, chin, and cheeks with the spoils of her campaign.

"Tory, oh, God." Leah's hand was on the back of her head, urging her to engage in the final skirmish.

She licked her slick entrance clean, then plunged her tongue inside.

"Yes," Leah hissed, lifting her hips and opening her legs wider. "Please, baby, I need to come so bad."

She lathed her tongue alongside but not touching Leah's turgid clit. She loved it when her normally bossy lover was reduced to begging.

"More," Tory growled.

"Anything. Anything you want. Just make me come."

"There are four more."

"No, don't stop," Leah pleaded as a bite to her thigh signaled Tory's retreat. "Oh!"

She gripped Leah's knees and flipped her over to attack the rear guard. She stalked her next victim, nipping and sucking upward from the ankle.

Leah squirmed as Donner quickly surrendered his post behind her knee, then grew still when Tory paused. With Tory's hot breath bathing the backs of Leah's thighs, she shuddered.

Comet had been spied.

Tory knew exactly why Comet was stationed on Leah's right butt cheek, inviting ambush. Leah loved Tory's teeth on her sensitive buttocks, relished Tory's assertive tendency to bite when they made love in this position.

"Look what I found," Tory whispered.

"God, I want your hand between my legs, your fingers inside me. I need you to make me come."

Leah jerked when Tory bit down hard on the hapless reindeer and moaned as she devoured Comet in one huge sucking assault. Tory's attack didn't stop with the tattoo. Leah writhed as Tory licked and nipped every inch of both cheeks.

"God, touch me before I come without it."

Tory stroked the inside of Leah's thighs, and Leah opened her legs in offering. When she stopped caressing her, Leah's hips pumped, as if begging for more.

"Please, baby. I need you. I need you now."

Tory didn't answer but pushed between Leah's legs and under her thighs. With her face pressed into the bed and her thighs draped over Tory's shoulders, Leah was totally open, totally exposed, and dripping wet.

"Oh, please lick me."

Again, Tory denied her. She worked upward to thrust her tongue inside, and Leah groaned. Tory inched her tongue higher and Leah's breath hitched.

"I'm gonna come. I'm gonna come." Leah was panting.

"Wait." Tory pushed up and covered Leah with her weight. She rubbed her swollen clit against Leah's firm thigh and filled her with her fingers. She stroked her inside and out, pumping her hand in rhythm with the rolling of her hips against Leah's leg.

Tory's orgasm gathered and began to swarm through her belly as Leah matched her movements, pushing backward to meet each thrust.

"I can't wait. I can't wait," Leah cried.

That's when Tory saw Blitzen, the last reindeer sentry, protecting the juncture of Leah's shoulder and neck—Tory's claiming spot.

"Now. Come now," Tory commanded, biting down hard and holding Blitzen in her teeth as she thrust with her hips and hand.

Leah's cries mingled with Tory's howl as they released together and rode out the waves of pleasure. They collapsed in a heap, their hearts pounding in perfect sync.

Tory lazily licked at the remnants of Blitzen and smiled to herself. Her very creative lover had so many facets to her personality that she looked forward to a lifetime of discovery.

She rolled onto her back and pulled Leah into her arms. They were both sweaty and parts of Leah still sticky, but Tory didn't care. She kissed her slowly, tenderly. "I love you."

Leah rose on her elbow, her eyes searching Tory's. "I love you, Tory." She combed damp tendrils of Tory's hair back from her face. "I don't like being away from you. I know we'll probably get better at it after a couple of years, but not now, not yet."

"I don't want to keep you from your work," Tory said. "I'm afraid you'd resent that somewhere down the road."

"I've already decided on my next project, and the research won't take me any farther than The Equestrian Center."

Tory frowned. "You're investigating our friends?"

Leah laughed softly. "No, sugar. Alisha told her daughter that I had a baby pony, and that's all the kid wanted to hear about. So, I told her a few stories about Sure's adventures and she said, 'You should write a book about your pony.'"

"You're going to write a kid's book?"

"You don't think I can?"

"I think you'd be wonderful at it. You're a natural storyteller." Tory grinned. "And you won't have to go away to do it."

Leah kissed her again. "No, I won't have to go away."

"I want you to move in with me." Tory blurted it out before she lost her nerve. "We can change the house any way you want, or we can sell it and build a new one." She stroked Leah's bare back. "I want to lie down with you every night and wake up with you every morning. When I'm working, I want to be able to think about you in your own office here, typing away on your laptop.

I want to cuddle on the couch and watch television with you. I want to do laundry with you, cook meals with you, take naps with you."

Leah's eyes filled and she laid her cheek against Tory's heart. "I've been waiting for you to ask."

Tory attempted to sit up. "Let's get dressed and go get your stuff now."

Leah pushed her back down on the pillows. "We'll go tomorrow. We're not done here yet."

"We're not?"

"No, sugar. I've got a big old red-nosed Rudolph that I saved just for you." Leah pulled the sheet back to expose all of Tory's long, naked body. "I just have to decide where I'm going to stick him."

Tory grinned. "Merry Christmas to me."

Read more of Tory and Leah's story in D. Jackson Leigh's novel Long Shot.

Touch the Stars

Bright points of light. Eyes of a million souls. Jewels nestled in a dark velvet blanket. The stars were too many to count. Just like her emotions were too tangled to sort out.

"How do you not feel adrift when you're up there, among the stars?" Alyssa asked, never taking her eyes from the night sky.

"As sailors have for a millennium, we use the stars to navigate," Jael said, her voice an anchor in the vastness.

Tomorrow, the next leg of their journey would begin. They would travel to the nest several mountains away, along with more than a hundred warriors hoping to bond with a wild dragon horse. To maintain as much secrecy as possible, they would hike through the Sierra Madre countryside, avoiding any settlements.

Tonight, however, was for them—she and Jael—before the demands of duty and leadership would take precedence.

Summer's warmth still enveloped the hilltop meadow even though the sun had set, and she wished she could hold this moment for eternity. She wanted to let the world save itself while she stayed safely tucked in the circle of Jael's strong arms. She closed her eyes, settled back against Jael's chest, and listened to Specter, Jael's dragon horse, tear the tender tops from the lush grass that surrounded them.

She opened her eyes again and the stars called to her. She

wanted to know what it felt like to be high above the earth, far away from the realities of their mission.

"Take me up there, Jael."

"Up where?" Jael placed a line of soft kisses along Alyssa's neck. Apparently her mind was focused on a more earthly pursuit.

"I want to fly."

"We flew up here."

She had flown several times, held tightly by Jael as she balanced them on Specter's back, but she'd always insisted they stay fairly close to earth because of the one-time attack of vertigo she'd suffered after a head injury. She was ready now to let go of her fear.

"I want to really fly, up there, high above everything where you can touch the stars."

A sharp nip made the muscles low in Alyssa's belly clench, and then Jael's teasing lips stilled. She hummed against Alyssa's neck. "That's what I love about you."

"What?"

"You have such a romantic view of everything."

Alyssa could hear the smile in Jael's voice. "I don't know what you mean."

"You can't actually touch the stars, silly. They're way above the breathable atmosphere. Not even Specter's wings can take us that high."

Warriors could be irritatingly rational sometimes.

As if he understood their words, Specter shook his head in agreement and then went back to his grass.

Alyssa turned in Jael's arms to smile at her. "I want to try."

"Are you sure? It's pretty high up." Jael's blue eyes were bright with surprise, even in the soft moonlight. "But it's amazing. The air is so thin that you feel breathless, but the wind currents are so strong, it feels like floating in a river." Her fingertips were rough against Alyssa's cheek. "I don't want to hurt you. If you feel even a tiny bit of vertigo, you have to tell me right away."

Jael's fingertips were capable of igniting into real fire. They also were adept at stoking a blaze of passion that burned through Alyssa so fast and hot that just thinking about it made her tremble. She kissed that clever hand. "I promise."

Specter left off his grazing and ambled toward them, apparently summoned telepathically by Jael. He extended his huge leathery wings, stretching them in the breeze. He seemed eager for the opportunity to soar. He nipped at Jael's belt and she nodded.

"Give me your belt," she said, removing her own. "We'll use them to fasten your legs to the base of his wings, so if we hit a rough spot in the air flow you'll be secured."

"Like a security harness?"

"Exactly. We'll use similar harnesses when the newly bonded warriors are first learning to fly their dragon horses, but I don't have one of those with me now. The belts will work just as well."

Alyssa frowned. "What about you?"

Jael chuckled. "I took a few unintentional sky dives when I was a beginner, but my legs are strong enough now to keep my seat during any of Specter's aerial acrobatics. Still, I wouldn't want to risk us sliding off if your full weight shifted against me."

She blinked at Jael. "You couldn't have fallen off. If you did, you wouldn't be standing here today."

Jael grinned and pressed her forehead against Specter's. Alyssa knew that touching made it easier for them to communicate. A mental image formed in Alyssa's head, too. Jael. Besides her pyro talents, she was a very strong telepath, and Alyssa appreciated that she was including her in their mental conversation.

Alyssa was suddenly looking down at hands clutching Specter's mane, the earth very, very far below them. The hands began to scramble for purchase and she felt jostled, then nothing but empty air, fast-approaching ground and overwhelming fear. Then Spector's broad back appeared under her, solid and warm.

When Jael drew back, Spector bobbed his head and curled his lip in a horsey laugh. Jael grinned, too. "That was the first time I fell off. Specter has always saved me, but I don't know if he could pick two of us out of the sky if we both slid off." She held up the belts. "So, we'll make sure you don't."

Alyssa hesitated, Jael's mental picture still fresh. She looked up at the stars, blinking, beckoning. Her desire to fly outweighed her fear. "Let's do it."

Specter stood very still, his perlino hide glittering in the moonlight. Jael strapped Alyssa's legs to his wings, then leapt onto Specter's back to settle behind her.

In tight quarters, Specter would rear and launch himself into the air, but the meadow was spacious so he cantered a short distance to lift off gently. His huge wings alternated power sweeps with gentle glides as he moved among the warm currents. They flew in wide circles until the ground was so far away, the trees and mountains were an dizzying, indistinct blur. Alyssa's stomach seemed to be eyeing her throat, and she swallowed several times to dissuade it.

"Don't look down. Keep your eyes on the stars."

Jael's breath was warm in her ear and Alyssa shivered, realizing the air had grown chill and thin. But before she could shiver a second time, warmth penetrated her clothes like a heating blanket against her back, and she chuckled.

"What's so funny?"

"Just thinking about when winter gets here." The fact that Jael could consciously turn up her body heat would come in handy during the winter months. "No need to drag out extra blankets as long as I'm sleeping with you."

She felt Jael's laugh rumble against her back. She was glad she hadn't been able to freeze the moment in the meadow, because she would have missed this one. Every minute of every day with Jael was precious. Alyssa tried not to think about what could be ahead for them. Jael was a warrior and would be in many dangerous situations.

"Stop worrying and enjoy this." A kiss brushed her cheek to punctuate the admonishment.

"Are you listening in on my thoughts?"

"You know I don't unless invited. You're just broadcasting so loudly, I can't help but hear."

"Sorry."

"I love that you don't shield me out."

Their relationship was a tightrope sometimes. Alyssa's empathic and Jael's telepathic abilities necessitated shielding to keep out the barrage of others' thoughts and emotions, as well as to keep from broadcasting their own indiscriminately. Only when they were alone could they completely relax. To do that was heaven. The downside, however, was that they each could tell if the other was shielding, so it was impossible to withhold anything when they were alone. The other could sense it.

Alyssa released her hold on Specter's mane and slipped her chilled hands into Jael's warm ones. The air grew balmy around them, and Specter canted his wings to hover in the jet stream. The stars seemed so bright, so close that she actually reached out toward one.

"It took me a long time before I gave up trying," Jael said, raising her voice a bit to carry over the force of the wind. "I finally became resigned to the fact that, no matter how close they seem, you can never really touch them."

"Never say never."

Another kiss to her cheek. "I'll qualify that then. In all my lifetimes, I've never touched the stars."

Specter tensed and Jael's arm tightened around her.

"What is it?"

Before Jael could answer, an angry scream split the night. Her ears were still ringing when Specter answered with his own dragon cry. A dark shape materialized out of the night, illuminated by a plume of red-yellow flame aimed straight for them. The jet stream diverted the flame to the left of them, and Alyssa released a scream of her own and grabbed Jael's forearms when Specter folded his wings and dove downward. She'd barely registered the abrupt drop when they were sideways and curling around the pursuing stallion in a tight circle. Even Jael reached for a handhold at the base of Specter's left wing.

Specter exhaled a long blue-white flame that licked at the tip of the Black's wing.

"Bero! Why is he attacking us?" She had to shout to be heard over continuous verbal exchanges between the two dragon horses. Their shrieks filled the air like two feuding tomcats, only a hundred times louder.

"That's not Diego's Bero. That's the wild stallion from the nest," Jael yelled back.

The two dragon horses leveled off and circled as they measured each other. The screams were deafening. She would have covered her ears if she hadn't needed her hands to grip Specter's mane. She wasn't going to be stargazing when they took the next sudden-death dive.

The Black made the first move, darting in and back with the agility of a hummingbird. He spit fireballs at them. Carrying the weight of two humans, Specter couldn't counter the Black's quick movements so he hovered and met each fireball with his hotter flame, exploding them before they could hit.

"Hang on," Jael yelled. "I'm going to help a little to scare this guy off."

She reached high above her head, both hands igniting into fiery orbs. Specter screamed, and Alyssa felt his ribs expand in a deep inhalation before he breathed a thick stream of flame. Fire shot out from Jael's hands and met Specter's flame to form a bright, blistering wall for several heartbeats before it exploded. The percussion blew back a wave of scorching air at them.

It was enough to discourage the challenger and he disappeared back into the night, one last scream echoing in his wake.

The acrid smell of sulfur followed as they descended to the meadow in a wide, gentle spiral. Specter, still jazzed from the battle, snorted short spurts of flame and, as soon as they dismounted, pranced away to punctuate his victory with a few celebratory bucks. When Jael slapped her hands together and pointed to the sky, Specter reared and screamed before launching himself aloft.

"He'll make sure the intruder isn't hanging around," Jael said, her eyes still scanning the sky.

"Jumping stars!" Alyssa had never experienced anything like that before. Her heart was still racing, her blood pumping. She was bursting with adrenaline and…and—

What hammered Jael stole her breath, nearly took her to her knees. In past lives, they called it battle lust—the unbridled arousal projected by Alyssa. But this was her sweet healer, newly anointed First Advocate of The Collective, the woman who only a few weeks ago was disgusted by their mission that would surely lead them into a war.

She took a deep breath. It had been a lifetime since she'd been part of any battle other than a practice skirmish with other members of The Guard, and she had been holding down her own throbbing reaction. She had no reserve to absorb Alyssa's. She searched for how to react. Alyssa couldn't possibly understand what she was feeling. "Are you okay?"

Alyssa's eyes were glassy with desire. "I am jumping awesome."

Jael took a few steps back when Alyssa stalked toward her. Did she even realize she was slapping her belt against her leg as she walked? What should she do? A quick jump with Tan, one of her Guard, had always been her way to take the edge off. But those encounters were rough and strictly physical. She couldn't be rough with Alyssa like she was with Tan, and there was certainly more between them than just physical release.

Alyssa stopped her advance and raised an eyebrow. "Tanisha? Really?"

"It was just blowing off steam." Dragon's balls. She must have been broadcasting her thoughts. She hadn't done that unconsciously since she was a fledgling. "And that was before you came along. Well, there was that one other time when you had me so hot I needed a cool-off."

"After you met me?" The playful smack on her leg with the doubled belt had a bit of sting to it.

"Ow. That very first day. You wanted nothing to do with me." She caught the belt as a second blow threatened and yanked Alyssa to her. She braced for the impact of Alyssa's body against hers, but not for the quick hook that swept her leg and landed her flat on her back in the grass. Alyssa's weight pushed all the air from her lungs when she free-fell with her and straddled her hips to grind herself against the closure of Jael's pants. They both groaned.

Her last thread of control gone, Jael fisted Alyssa's blouse and pulled her down for a bruising kiss of tongue and teeth. She pulled at the tie on Alyssa's pants. "Off. Get these clothes off." She was going to combust if she didn't have Alyssa's skin against hers.

Alyssa batted her hands away and jerked Jael's T-shirt up to expose her breasts. She fell on them, biting and sucking until Jael had to clench her thighs together to stave off the wave of orgasm gathering in her belly. "Off. Clothes off." The earlier demand was now a plea.

She lifted her shoulders and had started to raise her arms when Alyssa, still sitting astride her, worked the shirt over her head. But Alyssa had other ideas. She pulled the shirt down Jael's back before she could slip her arms out and pushed her back to the ground.

"You're never going to need Tan to touch you that way again."

Though the shirt at her elbows trapped her arms, Jael knew a dozen different ways to dislodge her captor and spring free. But the blazing desire in Alyssa's eyes—not the shirt—held her, wetted her thighs, and reduced her voice to a rough croak. "No. I won't."

Alyssa stood and quickly stripped her clothes off before ripping Jael's pants open and dragging them down her hips. The cool grass pricked at her heated skin, and her breath caught in her chest when Alyssa planted a foot on either side of her shoulders and stood over her. She spread her glistening sex for Jael to see. Stars. This woman was going to drive her insane. *Please, before I combust.*

Alyssa's smile was feral, and, for a second, Jael thought she would deny her. But she could feel Alyssa radiating her hunger as she opened her mouth to run her tongue along her lips in a teasing demonstration. Alyssa moaned and at last knelt over her. Jael bit her thigh in reprimand for making her wait, and Alyssa grabbed a handful of Jael's hair to force her where she needed her most.

She didn't know why, but it fascinated her that Alyssa's nether curls were the same deep red as her spiky crown. She tugged at the stiff hairs with her teeth, and Alyssa growled, her hips undulating to paint Jael's cheeks and mouth. Jael hummed as she relented and sucked at her. When Alyssa's legs began to tremble, she changed her point of attack and plunged her tongue inside. She strained against the shirt holding her arms, her fingers itching to replace her tongue, to push inside and claim her. In a small act of rebellion against the restraint, she moved up to suck again at her clit, swollen hard and pulsing, but clamped it between her teeth when Alyssa's legs began to tremble again.

Alyssa's hand tightened in her hair and jerked her away. Jael smiled at the pain in her scalp. She wouldn't have guessed such a tiger existed under Alyssa's peaceful zen. Nor would she have anticipated her little game of denial would unleash that tiger.

Alyssa straddled her hips again, grinding her plump clit against Jael. She grasped Jael's jaw, her fingers digging into her cheek, and bent to breathe her scream of release into Jael's mouth. Alyssa, her lover. Alyssa, the empath.

The force of Alyssa's climax slammed through Jael, bowing

her body and stealing coherent thought. Alyssa was all around her, touching her in places no one ever had, thrusting, claiming, driving her beyond any place she'd ever been, sucking her into a vortex. She couldn't sort the physical pleasure from the rush of emotion that was lifting her, filling her. Her ears rang with her own shouts. The stars pulsed and seemed to move in waves. She was flying. She was free-falling. She was dying. She was born again. She closed her eyes and drifted until she became aware of her own gasps for air and the frantic throb of her heart between her breasts. Then she smelled and felt the scorched grass under her hands and the soft fingers stroking her cheek. Alyssa's eyes, filled with worry, sought hers.

"Jael, honey, are you okay? I'm sorry. I didn't know…that's never…I didn't know that could happen."

Jael lifted her right hand and stared at it.

"Say something. Oh, please, I'll never forgive myself if I've hurt you."

The hard-bitten warrior in her felt light, floating in a sense of unfamiliar wonder. She met Alyssa's troubled gaze and struggled for the words to describe it.

"I…I think I touched the stars."

Read more of Jael and Alyssa's story in Dragon Horse War: The Calling.

THE POND

Willie Greyson sat on the weathered dock and extended her long legs out over the water. She dipped her heels, then immersed her feet in the sun-warmed pond. She wiggled her toes and frowned.

It seemed like she'd spent a lifetime at this small oasis hidden on the back part of Lori's father's farm, a lifetime of long minutes waiting for Lori to appear on the path across from the dock. They'd begun meeting here when they were just girls, Lori's hair in pigtails and Willie's in a single long braid. They were best friends. Willie fished and Lori talked. Damn, she could talk the paint off the side of a barn.

Then things changed. While Willie grew tall and lanky, Lori remained petite, her body softened with lush, womanly curves. Their relationship changed, too.

They discovered they wanted more.

Their first kiss had been at the beach. She borrowed Papa's truck and they spent the day sitting on the sand and wading in the surf hand in hand. They explored a rock outcropping, then stopped to rest in the secluded shade of a large boulder. They sat shoulder to shoulder, and Lori trembled against her. It was much too warm to be chilled, but Willie wrapped an arm around Lori's shoulders and pulled her closer. Lori looked up, their faces a hairsbreadth apart, and before Willie had time to think about it, she lowered her head and kissed Lori. Her lips were soft and warm and tasted faintly of the salt spray.

She drove home with Lori pressed against her side, until she pulled off onto a tractor path near Lori's house and stole another long, exploring kiss. That kiss left her breathless and hungry. But for what? Did other women have the same feelings for each other? She instinctively knew this was something they must hide, but it didn't stop them.

The kiss was followed by weeks, months, of more stolen kisses, tentative touches, and frustrated partings.

Willie wanted more.

She had a pretty good idea what "more" meant after one of their long make-out sessions had led her to a stunning discovery. She'd been confused by the dampness in her crotch afterward and surprised when it reappeared that night as she lay in bed and relived their kisses. She smoothed her hand down her belly and slid her fingers into her stiff curls. Yes, she was wet again. Was she ill? She didn't feel bad. In fact, it felt pretty good, really good when her fingers slid across her swollen tissue. A few more strokes and she experienced her first toe-curling, eye-opening orgasm. Wow. What had she done? Could she make it happen again? Did Lori know about this?

"More" became her new mission.

Lori was so beautiful. One look as she appeared at the edge of the pond's clearing and Willie wanted to bury her fingers in her thick mahogany curls. She wanted to stare into those sable-brown eyes framed by long, dark lashes and soak up the strength and shy affection she saw there. She wanted to feather kisses across the freckles that dotted Lori's otherwise flawless skin and to taste those soft lips.

She wanted that, but today she planned to have more.

Lori paused and their eyes locked. Willie was already wet from the anticipation, and Lori standing in the sunlight, barefoot and clothed only in a simple sleeveless gingham dress, made her shift to relieve the uncomfortable pressure building in her loins. The wood dock was hot against her own bare feet as she trotted to the pond's grassy bank and skirted the water to meet Lori under a huge shade oak.

Willie kissed her shyly, and the question in Lori's eyes told Willie that her nervousness was showing.

"I brought a blanket and swiped a jar of Papa's scuppernong wine," she said.

Lori smiled at the small feast Willie had spread out for them—wine, cheese, and soda crackers—and they sat with the food between them.

"Oh, Willie, this is wonderful. You won't get in trouble for the wine, will you?"

Willie grinned at her. "No, but one of my brothers might. Papa would never believe I did it."

Lori shook her head but smiled. "You're such a scamp. Your poor brothers, always taking the blame."

"They've all done it before, so they'll be too busy blaming each other to think it could be me." She uncapped the Mason jar, handed it to Lori, and watched her take a sip.

"It's sweet," Lori said.

"Sweet like you." Willie followed Lori's pink tongue swiping across her lips to gather all of the grapes' nectar. Her cheeks heated when she realized Lori had caught her staring, and she began to ramble nervously. "It won a blue ribbon at the county fair last year. Papa says this year's batch is even better, and he's going to enter the fair again next month."

Lori handed the jar back to Willie and lowered her eyes, toying with the hem of her dress.

Willie frowned. "What's the matter? Is the wine too sweet?"

"No, the wine is perfect." She looked at Willie, affection softening her gaze. "You're perfect." Her expression turned to frustration. "It's just that, well, Earl Montgomery asked Daddy if he could take me to the fair next month. I told Daddy I was going with you, but Mama said it's time for me to start paying some attention to boys."

Willie took a big gulp of the wine and swallowed it. "Is that what you want to do?" She stared at the blanket and picked at a loose thread near her knee.

"No." Lori crawled around the food and took Willie's face in her hands. "I want to go with you, Willie."

Willie searched her eyes and saw the truth of her declaration. "I told Papa I don't want to get married. I want to go to the university and get a degree and then a good job. I'll buy a house and you can come live with me. They'll call us old maids, but I don't care. I just want to be with you. I love you, Lori."

Lori's eyes filled. "I love you, too, Willie. Only you."

Her lips, her tongue tasted of the wine, and Willie drank her in. She gathered Lori in her arms and eased her down until they were lying side by side. She was careful though. Lori's tiny, delicate frame always made her feel big and clumsy. But Lori rolled onto her back and drew Willie down on top of her.

"I'll crush you," she murmured.

"No, you won't," Lori said. "I love the weight of your body on mine. I love your strength."

Willie kissed her way down Lori's neck and sucked at her pulse because she'd discovered that it made Lori hum with pleasure. She hummed now, and Willie reflexively pressed her tingling crotch against Lori's hip. She captured Lori's mouth, pouring all the passion, all the feeling that was welling up in her, into a long kiss as she inched her hand up to cup Lori's breast. They'd done this before, and Willie anticipated Lori's whimper when she circled her thumb around the rigid bump of her nipple.

She broke their kiss and stared into Lori's eyes as she slowly unbuttoned her dress. They hadn't done this before. They'd only groped and pressed together fully clothed. But Lori didn't stop her. Instead, she reached for the buttons of Willie's shirt, too.

Lori's chest was flushed, but her skin was cool. Willie slipped her hand under the stiff white cotton of Lori's bra, then closed her eyes and moaned at the supple flesh that filled her palm.

"Oh, Willie." Lori wiggled beneath her. "Let me up."

"I'm sorry, I'm sorry." She withdrew her hand and sat up abruptly. "I didn't mean—"

"No, it's okay." Lori sat up, too. "I just—" She unfastened the last button on Willie's shirt and dropped her gaze to take her in.

Willie had never needed to wear a bra under the work shirts she always wore. She was glad for that now. She shivered when Lori pushed the shirt back and trailed her fingertips lightly across her collarbone, then downward to touch her small breasts.

"So strong, but so soft," Lori said, pushing the shirt off Willie's shoulders. She stopped. "Is this okay?"

"Yes."

"I want…I want to feel your skin on mine, Willie. Take this off and unhook my bra for me."

Willie shucked off her shirt and leaned into Lori, kissing her again as she reached around to work the hooks loose and pull the straps from Lori's shoulders. Lori lay back and drew Willie down with her. Their moans mingled as their breasts brushed together.

"Willie." Lori's hands explored her back, her arms tightening around her.

Willie kissed her again. Their tongues danced sensuously, then desperately.

Lori squirmed. "Willie, God." Her tone went from breathless to desperate. "I want…I want—"

Willie knew what Lori wanted. "More," she said, smoothing her fingertips along Lori's cheek. "I want it, too. Do you trust me to show you?"

Lori trembled. "Yes. Yes, please, before I break into a million pieces from wanting you."

No one ever came to the pond except them, so Willie didn't hesitate as she rolled onto her back and unbuckled her belt. She could feel Lori watching as she stripped off her jeans and underpants, and when she rolled to face her again, Lori was wiggling out of her panties, too.

Clothes cast aside, no barriers between them, they both

stared. Willie thought she was going to faint at the sight of Lori completely naked, but then she remembered to breathe. "You are so beautiful," she whispered.

"Show me," Lori said softly.

She bent her head to taste Lori's lips, then her neck and chest. She flicked her tongue against one pink nipple, and Lori arched upward.

"Harder, Willie." Her hands were on Willie's breasts, massaging and tweaking her sensitive nipples. "Harder like this."

Willie gently clamped down on the nipple with her teeth and cupped Lori's other breast with her hand, lightly pinching. She smiled at her shy little Lori's full-throated moan.

She slipped her leg between Lori's thighs. Lori was slick and hot, and Willie groaned at the pleasure of knowing they were together in their desire. She kept teasing Lori's breast with her hand but rose to claim her mouth again. Her hips bucked and her sex slid easily against Lori's leg as their tongues moved together. Holy Mother, that felt good. Too good. Another stroke, and she'd be beyond holding back.

She skimmed Lori's soft belly to part her folds, and Lori whimpered as Willie found her swelling flesh. She'd had some practice now with her own body and used that knowledge to find the spot that made Lori wrench away from their kiss and gasp. She was careful to keep the pressure light, but it was difficult. Lori's thigh pushed harder into Willie's crotch, making it almost impossible to concentrate as her own need rode her hard, racing against her determination to bring Lori to orgasm first.

Lori sucked in an abrupt breath and her eyes widened. "Oh, God, Willie, oh." Lori's body bowed beneath her, and Willie gave in to her own climax.

She didn't remember rolling onto her back and pulling Lori on top of her, but she was thankful. Her heart surely would have pounded right out of her chest if Lori's cheek hadn't been pressed against it. They panted, perspiration sheening their naked bodies.

Lori shuddered, her body tensing and releasing with the residual of her climax. Her words were a breathy whisper. "I never knew."

"Yeah. Me neither." Willie stroked Lori's back, still marveling at the intimacy of touching her bare skin." She chuckled. "I sort of found out by accident one night after you got me all worked up with your kisses."

Lori lifted her head to hold her gaze. "I love you, Willie."

"I love you, Lori, more than I thought I could love anyone. It makes me crazy to think about you being with anyone else."

"I'll never love anyone but you."

Willie hugged her tight and swore she'd never let Lori go. They'd find a way to be together.

"Lorraine?"

They both jerked up as Lori's mother called out.

"Where are you?" Her voice came from the edge of the clearing.

"Shit." Willie looked for their scattered clothes.

"There's no time." Lori's eyes were wide with panic. "Jump in the pond."

They both ran to the water and dove in. When they surfaced, Mrs. Caulder was standing next to their blanket.

"Lorraine Caulder, what on earth?"

Lori bobbed in the water. "We were just swimming to cool off, Mama. Is something wrong?"

Mrs. Caulder stared down at their picnic and scattered clothes. "I'll tell you what's wrong." She put her hands on her hips and gave Willie a murderous glare that made her want to duck back under the water. "Your tomboy days of traipsing around the woods and skinny-dipping are over. You are much too old, young lady."

"But Mama—"

"No buts, Lorraine. Get up to the house. Now."

Lori gave Willie a beseeching look.

"Go ahead," Willie said, her voice low. She was beyond

miserable that their perfect afternoon had been shattered, but Lori's dilemma was what mattered. "I'll talk to you tomorrow."

Lori swam to the shore and quickly dressed. When she turned back to Willie, Mrs. Caulder swatted her on the butt. "Git. Now. Earl Montgomery has come calling and is waiting in the parlor. You need to get cleaned up before he sees you looking like a wild ragamuffin."

Willie lifted her hand in a silent wave when Lori glanced back for one last look before disappearing down the path.

Mrs. Caulder lingered, glaring at Willie, until she wondered if the woman expected her to get out of the water and dress in front of her.

"Y'all aren't children anymore, and you need to leave my daughter alone." She looked down at the blanket, and Willie felt suddenly exposed, as if Lori's mother could see what they'd been doing. Her eyes were hard when she looked up at Willie again. "I don't want to talk to your parents, but I will if you come around again."

Willie stood in the water for a long time after Mrs. Caulder left. She was scared, really scared. Could they keep her from seeing Lori? She waded out of the pond and dressed. Lori loved her. They would find a way to be together.

She waited at the pond every day for three long weeks—the worst weeks of her life. She closed her eyes to try to blank out the hollow ache that slowly choked her as she sat on the dock every day, waiting, wondering, and waiting more.

Desperate, she finally went to Lori's house, determined to talk to her. They could run away to another town and get jobs. She didn't have to go to the university. She'd do anything as long as she didn't lose Lori.

But when she walked into the yard, she could hear the angry voices inside. She knocked, but no one came to the door. She knocked again, and Lori finally appeared. Her eyes were red from crying, and she refused to look at Willie as she told her that she was going to marry Earl Montgomery next month.

Willie hung around until the day of the wedding and stood across the street from the church. When Lori arrived, she got out of the car and looked right at her, then walked into the sanctuary. Willie drove to the bus station, bought a ticket to Richmond, and joined the army.

❖

She never thought she'd find herself back at this pond, waiting once again for Lori. She squinted in the bright sunlight, searching the tree line again as if she could will her to appear. Every moment without her still seemed like a millennium.

Army life had been good to her, but even sweeter was their reunion and the years they finally spent together. The years of waiting had been more than worth it. So, there was no doubt that she would wait for Lori again…as long as it took. But then time had no relevance here in this oasis that was theirs.

The water shimmered around her, and Willie closed her eyes against the glare. When she opened them, Lori stood on the bank across from her. Her smile was soft. "Somehow, I knew I'd find you here."

Willie sprang to her feet and dove into the water, swimming across the small pond in strong, sure strokes. Lori waded in to meet her and they were in each other's arms again. Lori's kiss was as sweet as she remembered.

Then Lori's hands were on her face, smoothing down her shoulders and arms to cup Willie's hands in her smaller ones and examine them. She felt of her own face, then looked up at Willie in wonderment.

"We're young again."

"Yes." Willie held up her hands. "No more arthritis."

"I never minded. I was too glad to find you after all those years apart."

"I never expected I would go first. Was it hard after I left?"

"It was dark and confusing. Poor Leah. I don't know what

my granddaughter would have done without your great-niece to love her and help her through it."

"Tory is stronger with Leah at her side, too."

Lori nodded. "They'll be fine." She smiled. "Did you have to wait long this time, sweetheart? I couldn't keep track of the days. The dementia stole that from me, but sometimes I thought it was actually a gift because it kept me from knowing how long I was without you."

"It doesn't matter how long. I would wait all of eternity for you."

Lori looked around. "So, this is heaven? No angels or choirs? No judgment of our sins?"

"Are you disappointed?"

"Heavens, no. I'm relieved."

They laughed together, and Willie stole another kiss.

"Apparently, we must have done something right. We'll spend our eternity in the place where we shared our happiest memory." She gestured toward her offerings under the gnarled old oak.

Lori's smile went from sweet to brilliant. "Oh, Willie. In all the years I've loved you, I'm glad you never changed."

Willie winked at Lori. "I brought a blanket and a jar of Papa's scuppernong wine."

The story of Lori and Willie can be found in D. Jackson Leigh's Long Shot.

The Rider

My name is Marc Ryder. I ride horses for money.

I started out competing on the Grand Prix dressage circuit, but dressage felt too sedate, too controlled. So I jumped horses at Devon for two seasons, then wandered south and found brief respite from my restlessness on the polo fields of Wellington. The money was good and the competition fun, but I tired quickly of the Florida heat and decided to try steeplechase in Europe.

Steeplechase was exhilarating and reckless. But I was too tall and had to starve myself to be light enough to get the best rides at the top races. And, after a few years, the run-jump-run-jump grew repetitive, too.

Then, standing in Gatwick one day waiting for a flight to a race in Greece, I saw a real American cowboy. I took it as a sign because I am a professional rider. I sometimes ride airplanes to my next adventure.

So, I changed my ticket and managed to get a seat next to the guy. He was a rodeo rider, and we were headed to Texas.

I needed to put on thirty pounds of muscle to ride broncs and bulls, so I was relieved to be able to eat again. The novelty of a woman who could compete and win against the guys got me a lot of attention and several sponsors. I thought I'd finally found my calling until a particularly mean bull won me a long hospital stay and a leg full of metal pins.

That's how I ended up in the Dallas-Fort Worth airport, leaning on a cane and trying to decide whether I really wanted to board the plane to Cherokee Falls, Virginia. Home hadn't been on my itinerary for the past twelve years, but my former mentor, Skyler Reese, called to insist I return to the equestrian center to recuperate.

I had plenty of time, so I grabbed my duffel and settled on a bench to people-watch.

That's when I spotted her. Blond and blue-eyed, she wore the TSA uniform like it was tailored for her. Her shoulder-length hair and manicured nails kept her from being obvious, but something about the way she moved sent my gaydar pinging. I watched her direct the other security officers as they scanned the lines of people for possible terrorists and the carry-on bags for explosive devices.

She obviously was in charge. I like that in a woman.

Veteran flyer that I am, I know what triggers TSA suspicions. I purchased my ticket at the last minute. And, as I joined the impatient crowd filtering through the checkpoint, I pulled my ball cap low over my eyes and kept my sunglasses on. Also, I paused several times to let other people ahead of me. Even a rookie could tell I was maneuvering for the scanner operated by an employee spending more time talking than paying attention to his job. I could feel her watching.

I placed my duffel on the conveyer, threw my change and keys into a plastic tray, then limped forward. She was instantly at my side.

"Could you please remove your shoes and put them on the conveyor belt?"

I stared down at my Tony Lama boots as though baffled and then looked up at her. Her eyes were as blue as the Aegean Sea. I shrugged. "Can't."

"Everyone must remove their shoes to go through security."

"Can't you just X-ray them on my feet? I'll hop up on the belt and stick them under the scanner."

I was hoping for a smile, but her expression remained stoic. "No, I'm afraid we can't."

I tapped my cane against the brace wrapped around my left knee. "Pulling this boot off is a problem. I've got a bum knee. Can't bend it." It wasn't exactly true, but it sounded good enough.

"I'll get someone to assist you," she said.

Damn. I wanted her to assist me. Instead, she waved over a baby butch with a clip-on badge that identified her as a trainee. I hobbled to a nearby bench, and the girl kneeled to carefully tug off my boot.

Blond and Beautiful held out her hand. "May I see your ID, please?"

I handed over my driver's license. She looked at it, then back at me. I thought I saw her eye twitch. She was having difficulty hiding her impatience.

"Would you please remove your glasses and cap, Mr. Ryder?"

I pulled off my cap and released my shoulder-length dark hair that had been tucked under it. Then I moved my sunglasses to perch on top of my head and gave her a grin I knew would show off my dimples. Women love my dimples.

Her attitude changed from challenging to curious. "I apologize. Your license says Marc Ryder."

"My mother named me something awful, so I had it legally shortened to Marc when I turned eighteen. But everybody just calls me Ryder."

"Wow! You're Marc Ryder?" Baby Butch had returned from putting my boots on the conveyor. "Man, ESPN showed that bull stomping on you about a million times. When he tossed you up in the air…wow! Can I get your autograph? My friends are never going to believe I talked to you."

The kid obviously hadn't been trained yet in how to maintain that aloof TSA professional cool, so I held out my hand. "You have a pen?"

She patted her pockets but came up empty. Blond and

Beautiful was using a nice black felt-tipped fine point to write my driver's-license number on her clipboard, and Baby Butch stared hopefully at it.

"May I, Ms...?" I squinted at her badge. "Ms. Claire Simone?"

She reluctantly handed over the pen, and I scribbled my name across the bill of my cap that read EVERY SECOND COUNTS and handed it to Baby Butch. "Here ya go. I get these things free from one of my sponsors."

"Wow! Thanks."

Ms. Simone's eye definitely twitched that time. "If you would come this way, Ms. Ryder." She waved toward the metal detector. "Can you manage without the cane? It needs to go on the conveyor."

"I can manage if you help me a little." I was several inches taller, and she appeared startled when I flung my arm across her shoulders and leaned heavily on her. Truth was, I could walk very well without the cane, but she didn't know that. Christ, she smelled good. "What's that perfume you're wearing?"

"It's not a perfume. It's my moisturizer."

We paused to let a few other people rush through the detector first. I wasn't in a hurry to leave her company.

"Really? Where'd you get it? I need to buy a Christmas present for my sister." I, of course, didn't have a sister.

She hesitated. "Victoria's Secret."

I showed her my dimples again. "I love a woman who knows where to shop. What's the name of the lotion?"

She cleared her throat and mumbled, "Pure Seduction."

If I'd grinned any bigger, my face would've split. "It lives up to its name," I murmured in her ear before releasing her and hopping through the metal detector.

The alarms chirped in cadence with the happy pulsing of my clit, and I obligingly assumed the stance, my arms held out to the side while the security officer moved his wand over my body. It beeped at the old steel plate in my forearm and the new metal pins in my leg.

Ms. Simone raised an elegant eyebrow. Damn, that was sexy. I shrugged and she handed over my cane when it emerged from the scanner. "I'm afraid I'll have to ask you to come with me for a full body scan."

Oh, yeah. I would've loved a full body scan by her, but I had even bigger plans. I followed her to the new scanner that had been causing such a stir in the media but stopped short of stepping behind the screen.

"I'm afraid I have to refuse."

"The machine is perfectly safe. You would receive more radiation from—"

"I'm sure I'm way over my limit for the year." I tapped my cane against my leg again for emphasis. "I've had more X-rays in the past two months than most people get their entire lifetime."

She seemed to consider my point. "Then you'll have to undergo a body search or we can't let you board the plane."

I looked over her shoulder. "A female officer will do it, right?"

"Yes, of course—" She whirled to gaze at the officers currently on duty. All men. She looked at Baby Butch, who flushed and licked her lips. Ms. Simone turned back to me. "I suppose I can do it, since I'm the only qualified female here."

I sighed dramatically. "Okay, but be gentle with me."

A sharp look from Ms. Simone cut Baby Butch's snicker short.

The three of us crowded into a small room and she shut the door. "Could you remove your sweatshirt, please?"

The thick hoodie draped low over my hips and was bulky enough to hide an Uzi. So, it was more than adequate for what I was concealing. When I peeled it off and dropped it to the floor, I was immensely pleased to detect a faint hitch in her breathing.

Her gaze traveled over my tight black racer-back tank, and

my nipples came to attention, their salute more than obvious under the thin ribbed cotton. She glanced up and I gave her a sheepish smile and raised my arms for the anticipated grope. It didn't hurt that the position showed off the defined muscles in my arms and shoulders. I could tell she noticed.

She stepped back and looked into my eyes for a moment before dropping her gaze slowly down my lean torso. I cocked my hips slightly forward when she reached the bulge in my loose Wranglers. Her eyes jerked back up to my face and her expression shifted from amused to hungry. Oh, yeah. I'd read this one right.

She turned to pull two latex gloves from a box on the table. "Go to the supply room and get another box of gloves," she said to Baby Butch. "We're running low."

Baby Butch hesitated, glancing at the sign on the wall that read Two Officers Must Be Present During Body Searches.

Taking advantage of Ms. Simone's apparent fascination with counting the remaining gloves, I jerked my chin in the direction of the door. Baby Butch took the hint and smirked. "Yes, ma'am. I'll go to the one on Concourse B. It was just restocked."

We were on Concourse C, and I gave her a wink of approval as she made her exit.

"May I call you Claire? I like to be on a first-name basis with the women who feel me up."

She didn't answer, but I could see a hint of a smile.

She started with my hair, gently running her fingers over my scalp, then across my shoulders and down my arms. I guess I could've been hiding a knife or something explosive under my bare skin. I watched her face and wished she wasn't wearing gloves. I imagined her hands soft and warm on me.

She stepped closer to search down my back. When she moved to my front, I didn't even try to suppress my groan as she ran her hands several times up and down, pressing firmly over my hard nipples as required. She blushed an attractive pink.

I felt an answering flush rise up my neck, too, when she knelt and palmed my butt cheeks. I'm sure that little squeeze isn't standard protocol. Her hands moved quickly down the back and outside of my legs, then slowly up the inside of my thighs. I widened my stance and wondered if she could smell how wet I was.

I looked down to hold her gaze as her knuckles brushed my crotch and bumped against the contraband concealed there.

"Do you have something in your pocket, Ms. Ryder?"

"It's not in my pocket." I couldn't help that my voice had dropped to a low purr. She had that effect on me.

She stood, and my clit jumped again as she gripped my waistband and gently tugged upward as though measuring the weight of it.

"It's a...prosthesis," I explained. "There's no metal in it, so the easiest way to get it through security is to wear it. It's something I enjoy when I find the right person to share it with."

Her eyes darkened and she palmed the hard ridge, pushing it against my pulsing sex. "I'm afraid I'll have to confirm what it is, of course."

I couldn't stop the spasm that ran through my gut and thrust my pelvis into her hands. "I understand," I whispered hoarsely.

She slowly lowered my zipper and wrapped her fingers around the dildo's girth, pumping gently. I closed my eyes and whimpered, thoroughly blowing my smooth act. I'm not sure how she'd turned the tables so easily, but I prayed I wouldn't embarrass myself by popping off right there. I was so close. I blew out a breath as she withdrew and raised my zipper.

"Seems harmless," she said, fastening the button on my jeans but keeping her fingers tucked into my waistband.

I struggled against a sudden desire to kiss her, to plunge my tongue past her perfect lips. Instead, I confessed.

"I can guarantee it's not harmless," I said. "In fact, it has been known to cause...explosions."

The back of her hand subtly rubbed against my hard belly.

"Then this...prosthesis...may be something the TSA would like to research more. Do you live in the area, Ms. Ryder?"

"Just leaving. Going to Virginia for the short term. It doesn't mean I won't be coming back. Do you live here, Claire?"

She shook her head ruefully. "No. I live in D.C. I'm in town for another week to train staff on how to use the new body scanners." She stepped back, releasing me. "Enjoy your flight."

I shrugged. "I'm afraid I've missed my plane. It could be several days before I can catch another."

She looked at me, her blue eyes hooded. "I can recommend the hotel just down the road. That's where I'm staying."

I leaned so close our lips were almost touching. I could feel her breath on my face. "It sounds perfect, if you'll have dinner with me after you get off work."

"I suppose I could. There is that research—"

"And I'll be happy to assist you."

Did I mention I'm a professional rider? Sometimes I ride simply for pleasure.

SURRENDER

Marc Ryder struggled to secure the bright-red ribbon around the hat-sized box. Damn it. She could braid a shank of latigo into a halter or a hackamore in minutes, or tie a slipknot in a lariat in seconds, so why couldn't she tie a simple bow on an anniversary present?

She could have asked a more adept friend to wrap this for her, but this gift was very private. Even if she didn't tell them what was in the box, she didn't want anyone speculating or asking Bridgette about it later. Their deepest desires, how they shared their passion was only for them—an intimate secret shared between lovers. Not just lovers. Bridgette reached into her soul and put her hands on things Marc didn't even know she had inside.

That sometimes filled her with fear. If Bridgette ever left her, she'd be lost. Completely, utterly lost. She'd learned early in her childhood she should never depend on anyone else. Only herself.

So, she'd hopped from woman to woman since she kissed her first at fifteen years old. Love them and leave them. No ties meant nothing to lose. She thought her FAA friend Claire would take up the mantle, but she'd gotten an email just last week. Seems someone had finally clipped her free-flying wings, too.

Meeting Bridgette had sure changed Marc's world. She was instantly captivated, enchanted, ensnared by the bohemian artist with wild blond curls and mesmerizing hazel eyes. Surrender was her only option.

She smiled to herself. That's exactly what she had in the box. Bridgette's buried desire that she'd hinted at the week before. Surrender.

They'd flown to New York to attend an exhibit opening for a friend from Bridgette's art-school days. She said Kimberly Bergen had been a shy athlete whom she'd helped discover her artistic talent. Ryder thought they'd probably explored more than art, and, as ridiculous as it was to be jealous of something years before they met, it still needled her.

But Bridgette's best friend and gallery owner, Lydia, had raved about the exhibit, and Marc knew Bridgette was itching to spend a week in New York. After their first year together, Bridgette was still Marc's oasis, a drop of cool water on her parched throat, the nectar that made her barren desert life a lush garden. She would do almost anything to give Bridgette everything she desired. A trip to New York was simple enough.

Well, simple until they stepped through the door of Lydia's Manhattan gallery.

Bridgette wore a flowing emerald sari that was an exotic complement to the traditional tailored tux Marc wore. The tux was always a lustful trigger for Bridgette, but Marc felt totally upstaged when the featured artist greeted them in a vest and pants of black leather and heavy knee-high motorcycle boots that matched her studded wide leather belt.

Then there was the artwork. Apparently, the Breaking Bonds exhibit was a testament to the artist breaking out of her conservative upbringing to express her fascination with bondage. The contrast between the champagne-and-black-tie crowd and erotic depictions of BDSM, both on canvas and in sculpture, created a buzz of sexual tension that permeated the gallery.

"Bridgette! I've been watching the door for you since the moment Lydia confessed you were coming tonight." The tall,

dark-haired woman took Bridgette's hand to pull her close and kiss her on the mouth.

Marc was released from Lydia's hug in time to witness the kiss, and she growled.

Lydia linked her arm in Marc's. "Down, girl. Bridgette's heart belongs to you, and you need to give her a chance to explain that to Kim."

Lydia was right, but, damn, that other woman oozed sexuality and was putting her lips where Marc's belonged.

"Kimberly, it's so wonderful to see you. It's been, what, ten or twelve years?" Bridgette took a step back, her eyes shining with affection. "I knew the artist in you would one day find wings. I couldn't miss your opening."

Kimberly held on to Bridgette's hand, her gaze caressing every inch of Marc's lover. "You're as beautiful as ever," she said.

Bridgette blushed but extracted her hand to offer it in Marc's direction. Marc didn't hesitate, folding her fingers around Bridgette's possessively and stepping close. She met Kim's raised eyebrow with a challenging gaze.

Bridgette pressed her shoulder against Marc's. "Marc, this is Kimberly Bergen. Kimberly, this is Marc Ryder."

Kim stood a bit straighter, emphasizing her extra three inches of height over Marc's, but she stuck out her hand. "Kim. Only Bridgette calls me Kimberly. Are you also an artist?"

"An admirer of art." She wrapped her arm around Bridgette's waist, kissed her on the neck as only a lover would, and smiled at the faint shiver under her lips. "Or, rather, admirer of a certain artist."

"Behave," Bridgette murmured.

She turned back to shake Kim's hand. "Everybody just calls me Ryder." She offered up her cocky grin and automatically shifted her stance to slant her hips subtly forward. "I'm a professional rider."

Kim's eyes narrowed.

"Marc is an equestrian," Bridgette said before the posturing could escalate further. She pinned Marc with eyes full of love and smiled. "More importantly, she's my soul mate."

The air around them didn't move yet changed completely. She'd done it again. Reached right inside Marc and cradled her most fragile part.

Making a date for all of them to dine together before they left the city, Kim excused herself to circulate among the potential customers, and Marc and Bridgette slowly toured the exhibit.

Kim was, indeed, very good.

A series of paintings depicted a dominatrix with a variety of naked men, binding genitals, flogging, blindfolding and gagging, dripping hot wax onto bare skin, and, finally, cutting short, shallow slashes into the chest of a kneeling man, his cock swollen and blindfolded face lifted in blissful supplication.

There were female pairings, too, in different forms of bondage and torture, their faces undeniably infused with the pleasure their pain caused. Marc wasn't surprised that Kim's ability to convey that pleasure in obviously painful settings was translating into acclaim.

She was surprised, however, when Bridgette lingered before a life-sized painting of an angel blindfolded with arms and legs tied to the four corners of a rack while her wings were bound tight against her torso. A human female knelt between her legs, applying hand and mouth. Bridgette seemed so mesmerized, Marc slipped away to inquire about purchasing it for their upcoming one-year anniversary. She was disappointed to learn it had already been claimed.

Her disappointment turned into real regret when Bridgette's apparent fascination with the painting translated into a night of insatiable lust when they returned to their hotel room. She'd checked with Lydia again after they returned home, in case the buyer had changed his mind. No luck. The painting had been shipped. Lydia promised, instead, to pass along Marc's offer doubling the price the patron had paid Kim.

But it had been weeks and no word from Lydia, so she'd come up with a different idea. This damned bow, however, was confounding her.

Marc worked at the ribbon, but it wasn't coming out right. She frowned at the hat-sized box in her hands. The wide ribbon wasn't much different from the length of silk that was her bow tie. Bow tie! Why hadn't she thought of this before? She carried the package into the bathroom to stand before the wall-length mirror and tucked the box under her chin. Then she tied a perfect red bow.

She grinned. She was so super fucking awesome, sometimes she couldn't stand herself. Her grin faded a little as a tendril of insecurity wormed into a crack in her confidence. What if she'd read Bridgette wrong? What if she'd been wild that night because she was reliving her desire for Kim, the creator of the painting?

She fingered the bow she'd just tied. Maybe this was a bad idea. God, this relationship stuff was hard. She'd never worried before. If a woman didn't like what she did, what she wanted, she just moved to the next. What if Bridgette opened the box and said something like "you're kidding, right?"

...she is my soul mate.

She smiled crookedly at her reflection. That should pardon a few blunders now and again, shouldn't it? And if she hadn't misinterpreted Bridgette's interest—she wiggled her eyebrows at her reflection—the reward would be worth the risk.

Marc stood at the closed double doors to the studio where Bridgette had been painting all afternoon, her eclectic taste in music filling the cavernous studio and leaking through the walls. She paused and pressed her hand against the wood. Bridgette— her music, the smell of paint, the flash of her smile—had breathed so much life and light into this house that it no longer held the dark memories of Marc's childhood.

She was about to open the doors to that light when the sound of the doorbell stopped her. Damn. She needed a do-not-disturb sign for the front door. She knew Bridgette wouldn't hear the bell, so she put her gift next to the door and trotted downstairs.

"Got a delivery for Bridgette LeRoy." The man holding a clipboard drawled out Lee-roy with the accent on the first syllable like it was a man's first name. He eyed the doorway. "I reckon we'll have to lay it down long-ways to get it though this door."

Marc peered over his shoulder at a second man who was lowering a tailgate lift that held a wooden crate at least seven feet tall and two feet deep. Something that big had to be meant for Bridgette's studio.

"I've got a better idea. Wait here." She jogged through the house to the garage and hit the door opener to back her car out to clear the way to a freight elevator that had been installed when her artist grandmother had dabbled in sculpting huge blocks of marble for a while. They'd made use of the elevator when they'd pretty much emptied the house and remodeled it to claim the rooms as their own. A wheeled dolly stood ready when Marc keyed the doors open.

"Just move it from your dolly to mine, and I'll take care of it from here," she told them.

"You're my kind of customer," the man declared. "Sign here."

They were gone in minutes, and Marc looked at the address label taped to the crate. Connecticut. She shrugged. Bridgette knew people all over the world. The size of the crate was unusual, but receiving an unexpected package wasn't.

The lift doors opened and Bridgette turned toward her, brush in hand, her eyes questioning. She keyed the remote to silence the stereo as Marc pushed the crate into the middle of the studio. "Special delivery for Ms. LeRoy."

Bridgette smiled. "I'm not expecting anything." She rubbed her cheek against Marc's—careful not to touch her with her paint-covered hands and T-shirt—and kissed her lightly before turning back to the crate. "Wonder what it could be?"

Marc tapped the address label. "Recognize the return address?"

Bridgette's brow wrinkled. "No, I don't."

"Then I guess we'll have to open it to see." She guided it off the dolly and went back to the lift to get the pry bar she'd grabbed from the garage. She worked carefully to separate the front panel from the main frame because she realized the rectangular frame was thick and finished, unlike the rough wood of the front and back panels that was customary for shipping crates. Before she could puzzle over that, the front panel came free to reveal the angel, arms upraised and wings bound. Bridgette pulled away an envelope bearing her name that was taped to the side of the frame. She shrugged and shifted so Marc could also read it over her shoulder.

The painting is for Ryder. I heard she was desperate to procure it, I suspect as a gift for you. The crate, my lovely friend, is for you if you still desire it. If she truly is your soul mate, then she'll understand.
      Kim

Well, Lydia would have a little explaining to do, but she wasn't about to turn down the gift. She gently pried away the hard plastic inserts tacked to the crate to hold the canvas in place and lifted the painting out. The canvas was stretched across a frame less than four inches deep, so why was the crate two feet deep?

She turned back to find Bridgette flushed and staring at one corner of the crate where a thick metal eyelet was screwed into the wood. In fact, an eyelet protruded from each corner of the frame.

A mixture of thrill and jealousy slammed through her. It was as though Kim had been reading her mind, and she didn't want her to be hovering at the edges of their private moments. Forget Kim. This timing was too perfect to waste. She retrieved the box from where she'd left it in the hallway. When she returned, Bridgette was staring at the painting where Marc had propped it against the wall.

"Kim was right. Someone beat me to it in New York, but I had Lydia trying to buy it back so I could give it to you." She touched her fingers to Bridgette's cheek. God, she loved that face, those eyes that looked so deep into her. "It's an anniversary gift. This past year with you has been the most incredible adventure of my entire life."

Bridgette's eyes searched hers, her expression uncharacteristically uncertain.

Marc held the box out. "Kim may have helped with the painting, but this was all my idea."

Bridgette fingered the bow as if afraid to open it, then slipped the ribbon off and lifted the top. She stared at the contents so long Marc began to shift uncomfortably.

"Uh, I just thought…you seemed so fascinated with the painting at the gallery…but if I read things wrong, just forget it. It's not important."

"You weren't wrong," Bridgette said without looking up. She lifted one of the four fleece-lined restraining cuffs, fingering the leather.

Marc took a second one from the box, but when she moved to gently wrap it around Bridgette's wrist, Bridgette snatched her arm away and turned her back to Marc.

"Babe?"

She could see the fine tremble of Bridgette's body, her pulse beating wildly in her throat.

"I'd never do anything you didn't want, but you can share any need you have with me. Anything you want to explore. Any fantasy. If you desire it, then I do, too."

"Are you sure you mean that?" Bridgette's tone held a bit of warning.

"Always. Anything you want."

Bridgette dropped the box at her feet with a loud bang and whirled on her like an exploding bomb. Marc stumbled backward, but Bridgette's hand closed around the back of her neck, steadying her and drawing her forward. Her mouth was hot and rough, possessive and demanding on Marc's. She felt a leather cuff tighten around her wrist.

"You weren't wrong, love." Bridgette's eyes were bright shards of green roiling on a sea of stormy gray. "You just got it a little turned around."

Marc's brain was still reeling when a second cuff closed around her other wrist and Bridgette's hand was on her chest, guiding her backward. She stumbled at the edge, and Bridgette fisted the front of her T-shirt to hold her up until she found her balance to step up and back into the wood frame. She ran the straps of the cuffs through the eyelets overhead and tightened them so Marc couldn't move while she retrieved the shackles from the box. She hesitated, the restraints in her hands.

"Are you sure, Marc?" she said softly. "Are you sure you're okay with this?"

Okay? She was stunned. At times Bridgette took the lead in their lovemaking, but this was more, so much more. She was shocked at the heat in her crotch, staggered by the realization that her body hummed with the expectation of what could come next. She'd intended to fulfill Bridgette's wildest desires but instead had uncovered something she'd never considered in herself. Oh, she was no stranger to a little rough sex, but she'd always been the one in control, calling the shots, administering the pleasurable punishment. That had always aroused her, but this—helpless at the hands of the woman she trusted with her heart and soul—was beyond arousing. She raised her eyes to hold Bridgette's gaze. "Yes. God, yes. I think I'm going to come the minute you touch me."

Bridgette grabbed a fistful of Marc's short, dark hair and yanked her head back. "No. You're not going to come until I say you can. Do you understand?"

Marc moaned in frustration but nodded when Bridgette released her hair. She moaned again when Bridgette grabbed her crotch and squeezed. "Your safe phrase is 'I surrender.'"

Holy shit! She needed a safe word? Her hips jerked and she realized she was close, too close, so she concentrated on taking deep, even breaths. She could do this. She had enough physical control for precision show jumping at Devon. Enough command of her body to nail a polo puck between the goal posts from the back of a galloping horse. She could hold back something as simple as an orgasm. The ankle restraints took only a few seconds to secure, and Marc was pinned spread-eagle to the four corners of the frame.

Bridgette rolled her work cart over and rummaged through its drawer. Marc jerked when she held up a sculpting knife. Okay. This was her lover. Bridgette wouldn't do anything to really hurt her. She held her breath as Bridgette made several quick slices and her T-shirt fell to the floor. When she reached for the waistband of Marc's jeans, she yelped.

"Wait!"

Bridgette paused, but narrowed her eyes.

"Please. Not the jeans. These are my very favorite." They were worn to just the right softness, ripped in just the right places. "Please don't cut them."

Bridgette shook her head, a small smile twitching her lips, but knelt to release the ankle restraints and yank the jeans down Marc's slender hips and toss them aside to secure her feet again. Good thing she wasn't wearing underwear. Judging from the wild look in Bridgette's eyes, she might have torn them off with her teeth.

She looked up at her, nostrils flaring. "I can smell you," she said, trailing her nails up Marc's muscled thighs and making her shiver. "You like this, don't you?" She dipped her finger between

Marc's legs, scraping her nail along her hard clitoris. Her arousal glistened on Bridgette's finger and she licked at it. "Mmm. You're hard and tasty. You might need some help to keep from coming before I'm ready."

"I can come more than once. You know I can." Yeah, she was begging.

Bridgette went to the box again and held up the blindfold. "Perfect," she said.

Marc sucked in a breath as the black silk covered her eyes. The loss of her sight while helplessly bound formed a small pearl of fear in her belly, and she welcomed it. It was a familiar fear that triggered the adrenaline rush she chased when she approached a perilous cross-country jump or lowered herself onto the back of an angry rodeo bull. Her muscles twitched with anticipation.

Bridgette's breath was hot on her neck. "I have to gather a few things." Her nails dug into Marc's bare ass cheek. "Don't go anywhere." Her laughter echoed as she left the studio and entered the hallway, and then there was silence.

She waited, listening for Bridgette's return. After what seemed like long minutes, she yanked at the cuffs to test them. She was held tight. Damn. What if the house caught on fire or Bridgette fell and hit her head? She'd be helpless, hanging there. Unable to see or get free or call for help. Sweat trickled between her breasts and down her belly. As her anxiety rose, her flesh swelled. She instinctively tried to squeeze her legs together to massage the ache in her crotch, but the restraints stopped her. She whimpered and waited.

She was about to scream for Bridgette to come back, please come back when a hand closed around her right nipple and pinched. She gasped in surprise. Had she been so far inside her isolation that she hadn't heard Bridgette approach?

"Miss me?" Her voice was low, purring in Marc's ear. She pressed against her back. Bridgette was naked now, too. She embraced her from behind, both hands finding, torturing Marc's taut nipples. Her hands trailed lower, her nails playing over the sensitive muscles of Marc's belly, then abruptly plunged between her legs. "Yes, you did miss me." Her nails flicked over Marc's distended clit, and she bucked under the onslaught. "But we need to do something about that."

Fingers closed around her clit and pulled, and then something cold and hard pinched along the base. Marc hissed.

"It's a clit clamp. Ever used one?"

She jerked her head in a terse negative. It hurt a little at first. More like throbbed. Sort of a good throb. Like you want to come but can't, so you just hang there. God, she wanted to rub against something, anything to find release. She bit back a yell when Bridgette flicked her nail over the imprisoned tissue.

"You are so goddamn sexy." Bridgette thrust her hips against Marc's ass, leaving evidence of her own wetness. "Feel what you do to me?"

"Please. I'm dying."

"Soon, but not yet."

And then the air around her was empty. Bridgette's hands, her warmth, her scent were gone.

Marc listened intently as the music resumed, a low rhythmic beat full of tension, like the gathering before an epic battle. The wheels of the dolly rattled across the hardwood floor of the studio and down the hall. Her arms, shoulders, and legs were beginning to tire, but it was difficult to feel anything except the throbbing between her legs. After a few short minutes, the rattle of the dolly returned. There was a bit of shuffling and then rummaging in the big cabinet of art supplies. She could hear cans rattling on the cart next to her, liquids being poured and stirred. The throbbing had magnified to a pounding in her lower belly.

"What are you doing?" Her voice sounded tight and hoarse. "Bridge, please, I need you to touch me."

Bridgette's hands were suddenly on her face, her voice breathless and sweet. "You're my passion, my muse. And today, you'll be my living canvas." She yanked Marc to her, skin on skin, hot and demanding. Marc matched her tongue and teeth, lust and fire. Her clit strained against the clip squeezing it, and she gripped the leather straps of the wrist cuffs as her hips pumped impotently against air when Bridgette stepped back.

"Fuck." She yelled, her frustration boiling over. "Just fuck me."

"Trust me, I will before I'm done."

A wide, soft brush traced a torturous path in wide swirls from her rib cage, around her right breast, and over her shoulder to loop down her arm and around her bicep. Bridgette worked fast, her strokes strong and certain as though she was oblivious to the furnace she was stoking so hot, so fierce Marc was sure the paint would bubble on her flesh.

She began to shake when Bridgette moved to her left leg with a smaller brush, steadily working her way up from ankle to thigh. "Do not move," Bridgette ordered her firmly. "Or I'll have to start over again." She moved to her right leg, the wide brush again, making broad, looping strokes. "You're so damn beautiful. I love the way your thighs flex when I run the brush over them. I think about your thick, strong thighs when my eyes are closed and you're pumping into me."

Marc groaned. Bridgette's words stroked at her like a ghostly tongue, and her need rose with the crescendo of the music, pounding, throbbing, reaching for that climax.

The furious painting paused. "You like it when I talk dirty, don't you?" Her tone was light, as if she was casually asking which color to paint the kitchen. Then the bad girl was back. "You want to fuck me, don't you? You want to lay me down and push my knees to my chest."

Marc yanked at the restraints on her wrists. If she could only get free. She'd capture Bridgette, pin her to the floor, and fuck her until she screamed, until they both howled. No other woman could make her this crazy, this frenzied.

"Stop it."

She froze when fingers suddenly grabbed and squeezed her pulsing sex. A stroke, just one stroke would do it. But the fingers didn't move. She waited, her body reverberating with the drums that vibrated the air of the studio. Should she beg so she could be denied, or would silence push her lover into action? She bit her lip, powerless and suspended in indecision.

Slowly, Bridgette slid inside her. She dropped her head back, and her groan filled the spacious studio. Then her cry of anguish bounced off the walls and rafters when Bridgette withdrew.

"You're so wet, you're dripping on my artwork." She slapped Marc's muscled ass. "I think you should be punished for that."

Marc braced for another slap and was caught off guard when, instead, a clamp closed around her tender right nipple, then her left. She gasped at the bite of pain and growled at the light tug that shot a bolt of pleasure straight to her groin.

"You're so fucking sexy, I want to take you now."

"Yes, please."

"But I have to finish."

Groan.

Frantic fingers, not brushes, dabbed and swiped streaks of cool paint along her ribs and down her arm. "Close your eyes and do not open them until I say." The blindfold was gone and Bridgette began to work on her face. She could feel her, the heat of Bridgette's body inches away, and it took every bit of her control not to open her eyes and savor the naked body she knew so well. As if reading her mind, Bridgette gave the nipple clamps another small tug. "Closed until I give you permission." She worked in silence for another minute. Marc's arms and legs were starting to shake, the muscles cramping.

Then she stopped. Marc could hear her circling, feel her breath on her neck. "You're magnificent," she whispered. "Open your eyes before I get back, and I'll make you hang there and watch while I pleasure myself." Her voice was commanding now.

Marc shivered at the image, scrunching her eyes tight. She needed to touch Bridgette. She needed Bridgette to touch her. Her nipples and clit had gone numb, and the pounding in the groin was nearly unbearable.

She barely registered the rattle of the dolly wheels across the floor and down the hall, but her senses zeroed in on the sound of its return. It stopped in front of her.

"Open your eyes."

She squinted in the sudden brightness, then nearly jumped out of her skin at the fierce creature before her. She blinked and the creature blinked back. She was staring at her own reflection.

One side of her face was painted in sniper camouflage, the other side in Apache war paint. The right half of her torso was covered in the blue swirls of a Celtic warrior, the left in tiger stripes. A black dragon curled up her leg to her left thigh, and African tribal designs covered her right.

"This is what I see when I look deep into you. A warrior. Wild and fierce and so proud." Bridgette moved toward her, drying her hands on a towel and wiping at the drips and streaks of paint that were evidence of her work. Her eyes were hungry as she prowled closer, her blond mane loose. Lioness. "And I've captured you."

Marc growled and lunged, only to be brought up short by her bindings. "Bridgette!" She yelled at the rafters, struggled against the cuffs. Then Bridgette was on her.

She gasped when the nipple clamps released and blood poured back into the tortured tissue. Then Bridgette was on her knees, her fingers pumping into her, filling her. Movement caught her eye, and the reflection of a beautiful, naked goddess between the legs of a savage, yet helpless, warrior drove her instantly to the edge. Then Bridgette's teeth closed around the clit clamp and pulled it free. Her tongue, hot and tender, licked at the flames burning up her legs, through her belly and screaming through her lungs. Her breath stuttered in her throat, and she strained against the leather that held her until the fist of pleasure in her gut released her to breathe again.

Marc slumped, dangling from the frame. Holy Mother. She wasn't religious, but that sure felt like a celestial experience.

Bridgette was careful to hold her up as she released the

bindings, then gently guided them to the floor, where she cuddled against Marc's side.

"We've been together an entire year, Marc, and you never hinted that you liked a little pain," Bridgette said quietly.

Marc stared up at the ceiling, absently running her hand along the familiar curve of Bridgette's hip. "I didn't know I did." She struggled to put her feelings into words. "I just didn't expect—"

Bridgette rose up on her elbow, worry furrowing her brow. "If you didn't want to—"

"It was incredible."

Bridgette's face relaxed into a small smile. "It's not something I'd desire often, just when I'm in a particular mood."

Marc nodded. She felt the same. "So, while we're confessing, you never told me you had a dominatrix fantasy."

Bridgette blushed. "A fantasy is all."

"Never tried it before? Not even with Kim?"

Bridgette shook her head, holding Marc's gaze so she could see the truth in her eyes. "Kim knew I was interested because she found some drawings I did when we were in college. I've never trusted anyone enough to try it…until you." She nipped hard at Marc's lip, her eyes bright. "I knew you could stand up under siege. You're magnificent." She rose up on her knees and twisted Marc's tender nipple. "Up."

Marc groaned. She wasn't sure she had the strength to stand. "I surrender."

"Not just yet, soldier," Bridgette said. "Your tour of duty isn't over." She grabbed Marc's hands and pulled her to her feet. She shivered as Bridgette traced the blue Celtic swirl on her shoulder. "You might be my best work yet."

She turned and extracted one last item from Marc's box. "Spread 'em."

Marc obediently widened her stance. She was hard the instant Bridgette held up their favorite double-ended cock and sucked in a breath when Bridgette rubbed it against her still-sensitive sex.

She was slick with cum and moaned as it easily filled her, and again when Bridgette activated the vibrator encased in the pliant silicone.

Bridgette dropped to her knees to tighten the harness and leered up at Marc as she pumped it a few times. Damn, she thought she was spent, but another few jerks and she was going to blow again. She grabbed Bridgette's wrists and yanked her hands away.

Marc looked up and grinned at her macabre reflection. The tide was about to turn in this siege. She hauled her kneeling lover to her feet.

"Time for the cavalry to mount up."

Read Marc and Bridgette's full story in D. Jackson Leigh's novel Every Second Counts.

WIGGLE-WIGGLE-WOMP

The soft slap of my sneakers echoed rhythmically in the silence of the third-floor corridor ringing the coliseum. Except for the occasional straggler looking for the VIP lounge's free beer, the hallway was empty, just the way I felt.

We always came to the basketball tournament together. It was the highlight of our year—four days of beautiful, athletic female bodies, gladiators of the court pushing their abilities and opponents as far as possible. We both loved the competition, the cheering, the greasy hot dogs and roasted pecans. We loved getting to know the people sitting around us, strangers at the beginning and new friends by the time the tournament ended.

Sure, plenty of those tournament friends, as well as our personal friends, filled the generous seating this year. But she had to work over the weekend, and her absence licked the red off my candy, spoiled the milk in my cereal, let the air out of my fun. We always came together. I wanted to whine but settled for a silent sulk and another solitary trip around the coliseum's circumference.

I glanced up at the periodic TV monitor near the end of my fifth lap. The next game was about to begin. I sighed. The friends I was sitting with would wonder where I'd gone. First, a pit stop. I pushed through the door to the ladies' restroom. The top-tier seating wouldn't fill up until the last two days of the tournament, so there was no line. Just empty stalls.

I was about to flush when I heard the door open and someone come in. I expected it to be one of the bored spouses cajoled into attending the tournament because her partner loved basketball. The VIP lounge was usually filled with them, drinking the tournament away while their more sober partners were downstairs actually watching the action.

When I exited the stall, the newcomer was leaning against the row of sinks, playing with a tiny toy badger. She was really cute—short black spiky hair and blue, blue eyes. I'm a sucker for blue eyes. She pressed the badger's hand and set it on the long vanity. It shook its furry little butt as it inched along the sinks. "Wiggle-wiggle-womp," it growled out in a grumpy old-man voice before reciting a plug for a local car dealership.

I smiled at her. "Cute."

She looked up from the toy and cocked her head. "You think so?"

I shrugged. "In a weird kind of way, I guess. Where'd you get it?"

"I saw it on a local TV commercial, so I went to the dealership and bought one."

"Huh. Didn't know they sold them. The commercials are pretty popular, though."

"So, you live here?"

"Not in Greensboro, but only about two hours away." I dried my hands and took aim at the trash receptacle. The wadded paper towel arced perfectly across the room and joined the rest of the trash. "We're all about basketball in North Carolina."

"Three points," she said, acknowledging my score. "Then you can be my first test subject." She held out her hand. "I'm Haley."

I smiled and took her hand in mine. "I'm Logan."

"Pleased to meet you." She held up the toy. "Interested?"

Not in that toy. I dropped my gaze in an obvious sweep of her toned body. "In being your test subject?"

Her face reddened, but she grinned at my response. "Yes. I'm working with the WNBA to put together marketing profiles for two new expansion teams. One of the locations under consideration is Portland, Oregon. So, I'm thinking the Portland Badgers." She squeezed the badger's hand again, and we watched its butt wiggle as it chanted its slogan. "I was thinking there must be a way to work that wiggle-wiggle-womp into our marketing material."

"You're kidding, right?"

She raised her eyebrows. "No. I'm totally serious. I can see it now. The Badgers make a really big play, and the fans stand up, turn their butts to the opposing team, and—" She pressed the badger's hand a third time and turned around to demonstrate. "Wiggle-wiggle-womp. Wiggle-wiggle-womp." She chanted along with the toy and shook the cutest ass I'd ever seen.

After I unswallowed my tongue, I began to laugh. The more I laughed, the more she performed.

She finally stopped and turned back to me. "See? You love it."

I nodded enthusiastically. "I'm ready to buy season tickets."

She winked at me. "Thanks for the input."

"Are you going downstairs?" I hoped, I hoped. "The next game must have started by now, and I have an empty seat next to mine."

She shook her head. "I've got some business to take care of, but maybe I'll see you around later." She picked up her furry friend. "Enjoy the games this afternoon."

Then she was gone, and I was left with nothing but the throb between my legs. I briefly considered ducking into a stall to take care of that. Two minutes max. Instead, I decided to enjoy the sweet ache as a reminder of her dance and the possibility I might see her again.

❖

The throb was in my ears now, the pounding in my head.

I usually loved the after-games parties. Drinking and dancing and drinking. It was the one time each year we sprang for an expensive hotel room so we could attend the raucous lesbian gathering downstairs and just stumble upstairs to fall into bed.

My heart, however, wasn't in it tonight. My girl wasn't here. No slow dances. No stolen kisses. No dark-corner groping. It sucked the life out of my party.

I stirred my drink and sank deeper into my pout. My friends were getting obnoxiously inebriated. The disco-themed music was too loud, and the alcohol in my drink was making my sinuses swell. I wondered if my friends were drunk enough for me to slip up to my quiet room, where I could lie in the dark and mourn my ruined vacation.

"Is this seat taken?"

I turned and fell into those Carolina blue eyes, completely forgetting that I'm a die-hard Duke fan. The night suddenly didn't seem so dark.

I grinned at her. "I was holding it for you."

She waved at a waitress carrying a tray of drinks. "Over here," she said.

The waitress unloaded two tall cranberry and vodkas and eight shots of buttery nipple, then disappeared with a smile and a ten-dollar tip.

"I call this 'sweet-tart,'" she said, smiling at me.

I looked over the selection of drinks, then at her. "Uh, Haley, right?" Damn, she had cute dimples.

"That's right." She divided the drinks between us and held up the first of her four shot glasses. "To the Badgers."

I grabbed a glass and downed it with her, then sipped my Cape Cod. She was right. The sweetness of the butterscotch schnapps was a great contrast to the tart cranberry juice. She was sweet to buy the drinks for us, and the alcohol left me feeling like a bit of a tart. I lifted a second shot. "To the bluest eyes in Carolina."

She downed the second with me and grinned as she picked up the third. "To tall, sexy Duke fans."

Oh, yeah. The vacation was saved. The song segued into an old Donna Summer tune, and I made a final toast. "To bad girls."

We tossed back the last of our buttery nipples, and I took a big gulp of my Codder before she grabbed my hand and led me to the dance floor. Four songs later the only thing pounding and swelling was between my legs. My blood pumped with the music and the sway of her hips. My eyes followed the tiny drop of perspiration that trickled down her temple and along her jawline, then stopped at her very kissable lips pursed in concentration as she danced. Those lips were moving now. She was talking. But my ears, my thoughts were filled with bad girls, and I only blinked at her.

So, she gestured as though she was drinking something and led me back toward our table. We were winding through the crowd when a drunk stumbled into a waitress with another laden tray. I whipped an arm around Haley's waist and tried to yank her out of the way, but the drinks hit her thighs and soaked her pants down past her knees.

"Sorry," the drunk muttered before staggering off.

"I'm so sorry," the waitress said. "Let me get you a towel."

Haley looked down at her dripping pants. "I'm not sure a towel's going to be much help."

"I have a room upstairs," I offered. "I'm sure I have some sweats I can loan you."

"Really? That'd be great," she said.

I took her hand in mine for our walk to the elevators and didn't relinquish it even when others crowded in with us or when I had to dig my room key from my pocket and unlock the door.

She turned to me as soon as the door closed. Our eyes met and she touched my cheek. Her lips tasted of cranberries, her tongue of butterscotch. She moaned, and I'd swear the national anthem was playing as she fumbled with the buttons on my shirt. Was that the starting buzzer sounding in my head? Play ball.

We struggled with each other's clothing, but I won the toss, coming away with her pants. I passed them off to the chair and walked her backward to the bed to set up the play. She yanked me down on top of her in a woman-on-woman defense, but I blocked her attempt to get a hand down my pants and managed to steal her panties.

I was ready to make my play.

I drove right down the middle, laying nips and kisses down her neck, pushing her T-shirt up to taste her breasts and belly, and leapt forward when I found the lane wide open. She was hot and swollen and salty-sweet on my tongue. Her moans filled the room. Her defense was failing. I could have scored easy points. Instead, I eased back to use up more of the clock.

She writhed under me. "Please, I need to come."

The shot clock was running close, so I went for the score. I let my teeth scrape along her turgid clit as I sucked her in.

"Oh, oh yeah." Her eyes went wide and her body rigid when I filled her with my fingers to show her my best stroke. Her body bowed and she screamed.

Score. We both panted from our exertion.

She pushed me back and tugged at my pants. She had possession now and apparently wasn't ready to call a time-out. I love a woman with stamina.

I realized that, although my shirt was half-unbuttoned and my pants hanging open, I was still dressed. "Off," she said.

I stood and dropped my pants and underwear to the floor. I was so ready, my stomach clenched. I moved to straddle her shoulders in hopes that she'd take advantage of the open court and go for the fast break, but she had other ideas.

She grabbed the front of my shirt, jerking me to the bed. A clear foul, but I liked her physical play. She rolled me onto my back and ripped my shirt off, buttons flying across the room. Okay. That was definitely a charging violation, but her mouth covered mine and swallowed my protest.

A fast break was definitely not in her plans. She took her

time, exploring my mouth with her tongue and my body with her hands. I shivered when she licked my pulse and dragged her nails low across my belly. I shuddered when her teeth clamped down hard and her tongue flicked against my taut nipple. And I whimpered when her fingers began to stroke where I needed her most.

God, I needed to come. I bucked my hips to encourage her to stroke harder, faster, but she bit down on my shoulder and flung her leg across my thighs to pin me to the bed. She was setting the tempo now.

Then she stopped. "Time-out," she said, releasing me and jumping to her feet.

"Wha-what? Where are you going?" I was rattled. Did I drop the ball? Miss a call?

She grabbed her pants and ran into the bathroom. "I don't want these stains to set. These are my favorite pants."

I could hear water running. Seriously? I'm lying here with my clit hanging out and so near the edge. I slide my hand down my belly and into my soaked curls.

"DON'T TOUCH YOURSELF."

I jumped when she yelled. How did she know? She couldn't possibly see through the bathroom wall. I rolled onto my side, but she returned to slip in behind me before I could box her out. I was bigger and stronger, but she had momentum on her side and rolled me onto my stomach. Before I could regroup, her thumb was inside me, and her fingers slid over my clit.

"Oh, fuck." Her hand was ice-cold against my overheated sex, and the contrast was strangely arousing. Her inside-and-out, inside-and-out game was perfect, and she finished me off with a slam-dunk that made me bury my face in my pillow and scream.

Game over. She'd definitely bested me.

She pulled out slowly as she peppered consolation kisses across my shoulders. She smoothed her hand down the arch of my back and over my bare ass. "I can see a lot of potential here," she said, stroking my glutes.

"What? Wasn't that enough of a spanking you just gave me?"

"Mmm. The score was close, but I think I won." She climbed off the bed, and I flopped onto my back to watch in fascination. She still wore her T-shirt, but it wasn't long enough to completely cover her cheeks as she ducked back into the bathroom. She reappeared a moment later with her rinsed pants on a hanger and crossed the room in front of me to suspend them over the heating unit by the window.

I smiled. "I can see your butt."

She looked over her shoulder. "You like that, don't you?"

I wiggled my eyebrows. "Yeah. Very sexy."

She finished hanging the pants to dry, then winked and turned her back to me again. She wiggled that incredibly cute ass. "Wiggle-wiggle-womp."

I groaned, and she teased me with a series of wiggles.

"Lucky for you," she said, "this is a double-elimination tournament." She tugged her T-shirt off. "Let's see if you can win this round." She climbed onto the bed and straddled me. "Then we'll be forced to hold a play-off to determine the winner."

"Sounds like a win-win situation to me," I said happily.

❖

I pulled into the driveway at home and sighed. The tournament was over again until next year. My team hadn't won and I'd missed cheering next to my girl, but it was still the best tournament experience I could remember. I smiled at the memory of Haley and waking up the next morning to an empty room and the badger staring at me from the pillow next to mine. "Relax and enjoy the rest of the tournament," the note said. I plucked him from his spot on the dash of my truck, grabbed my duffel, and went inside.

"Honey, I'm home." Her car was in the driveway, so she was here somewhere.

"Hey, baby, did you have a good time?" Her muffled voice came from the laundry room.

"Probably the best tournament ever," I said, placing my little badger buddy on the kitchen counter.

"Throw your duffel in here, and I'll add your dirty clothes to the ones I'm washing."

"Why don't you come out here first? I brought you a little present." I could almost see her rolling her eyes, sure that I'd brought home the hundredth free basketball T-shirt they throw out into the crowd at every tournament.

Still, she dutifully appeared, and I pulled her into my arms for a long kiss.

"Wow," she said, when I released her. "I thought you'd be pouting because our team lost the final."

"Nope." I grabbed the badger and held him up. "I brought you a souvenir."

She took him, and I dropped my hands lower to cup her butt. Yeah, I'm an ass woman, for sure. She squeezed his little hand, and I palmed her firm cheeks when he growled out "wiggle-wiggle-womp."

She wiggled her eyebrows at me and I laughed, feeling so free and relaxed and loved.

"But Haley…really? That's the name you came up with?"

"She's your favorite player. You've been drooling over her all season."

"She's a twenty-year-old child, and I only drool over you."

I kissed her again, then drew back and looked into those Carolina blue eyes that could almost make me forget I'm a die-hard Duke fan. "I'm going to have to work hard to top that little role play."

She laughed. "You liked it, huh?"

I tossed my duffel into the laundry room and stripped to throw my clothes in after it. Then I winked and turned my back to her and wiggled my ass. "Wiggle-wiggle-womp," I said, sprinting to the bedroom with her hot on my heels.

FIRST KISS

Jamie carefully removed the tight band from the knob of braided mane, tucked it in her pocket, and unraveled the twisted strands to smooth them along the horse's neck before moving to the next. Tommy led the last of the horses they had taken to the Cherokee Falls Annual Hunter & Jumper Competition past Jamie and tied it to the hitching rail behind her.

"Leave him, Tommy. I'll take care of him."

"I don't mind," he said, coming around to peer at her from the other side of her horse again. He flopped against the hitching rail, reminding her of the scarecrow in *The Wizard of Oz*—all arms and legs. "You've already done six of 'em."

"I'd rather you see if Sky needs help with the other kids getting their horses settled." He was at least two inches taller than her five-foot-eight since his last growth spurt, but she was two years older and outranked his equestrian accomplishments. "I'll be heading off to college in another year, and Sky will need you to help with the younger kids." The children who participated in Skyler Parker-Reese's Young Equestrian Program came from troubled circumstances and brought a lot of problems with them. Most came and went. Some, like Jamie, stayed and helped with the new kids. "I'm counting on you to step up and watch her back."

The boy straightened. "Sure, Jamie. You know I will." He

hurried into the barn where Skyler was supervising the bathing of horses before they were turned out in the late-afternoon sun to dry before dinnertime.

Jamie returned to her task, slowly unraveling the braids to drag out the task as long as possible and keep watch over the large outdoor ring where a slouching handicapped young man rode astride the equestrian center's old matriarch mare, grinning as he clung to the saddle's horn. Two volunteers walked on each side of the mare, ready to catch him if he shifted wrong.

Jessica Parker-Reese, Skyler's wife, who had added the therapeutic riding program to the center, sat on the tailgate of a pickup with a woman Jamie recognized as the handicapped teen's mother. The women laughed and waved when the teen called to them from his perch on the mare. But that happy scene wasn't why Jamie lingered over a task she normally would complete in minutes.

Her gaze settled on the slim figure leading the mare around the ring, and Jamie frowned. She untangled the final few braids on the gelding's mane, then used her pocket knife to snip the bands on the second horse's braids. She was done in two minutes and called into the barn. "Yo, Tommy. Can you give me a hand?"

Tommy reappeared.

"Can you take these two in the barn and then come back to get Summer? I think they're about done in the ring, but Ellis looks like she might need help."

To the casual observer, the young woman appeared to step with only a slight limp as she turned a blazing smile up at the young man on the horse. Jamie saw something different. She recognized the odd twist in her friend's gait and the stiff set of her shoulders.

Tommy saw it, too. "Dang it. She'd fall over before she'd admit she was hurting."

The three of them were the oldest of the students in the Young Equestrian Program. Jamie, seventeen, was the leader, and Tommy, fifteen, her right hand because of his similar equestrian skills. At sixteen, Ellis was the middleman. Even more, she was the glue that held them together, their calm anchor when things grew stormy.

But Ellis had been born with her right leg twisted so badly her foot nearly pointed backward. She bore the physical scars of many surgeries and the emotional scars of cruel childhood teasing. Even so, she always seemed to have a kind word, a reassuring hug, or a bright smile for whoever needed it.

Tommy led the horses into the barn and Jamie struggled to stroll casually, rather than jog, to the outdoor ring. She waved Ellis over.

"If you guys are about done here, we can put Summer in the wash lineup with the other horses. They're down to the last few and won't notice one more." She smiled up at the young man. "How'd it go, Jer?"

Jerry suffered from multiple sclerosis and was a regular at the center. "Fantastic. I look forward to this all week."

Jamie hesitated, glancing briefly at Ellis. "If you guys aren't finished, how about I lead Summer around once so you and I can visit a bit?"

Jerry glanced at Ellis, then winked at Jamie. "I wouldn't normally turn down a walk with a second young hottie in the same day, but I'm pretty tired. I think I'm done."

Jamie smiled. "Let's get you down, then."

One of the electric golf carts used for quick transport between the sprawling center's five barns and fitness facility slid to a stop, and Skyler hopped out. Tall and blond, she still moved with the athletic grace of a gold-medal Olympian, although now she mostly spent her days training horses for other people, supervising young equestrians, running the equestrian center with her wife, Jessica, and chasing after their two-year-old daughter. She looked up at Jerry. "How about a ride to your truck? Easier than getting that wheelchair through this soft turf."

"Sounds good to me," Jerry said.

"Jamie, you've got his feet." Skyler expertly slid Jerry from the saddle, locking her arms around his chest while Jamie lifted his legs, and they easily carried him to the cart and belted him in for the short ride. When Jamie leaned over him to adjust his feet in a comfortable position, he put a hand on her shoulder.

"Ellis is hurting, Jamie. Take it from a guy who spends a lot of time covering up pain. Get her up to the training center. A good soak in the whirlpool will help, okay?"

"He's right," Skyler said, sliding into the driver's seat. "Help me get Jerry into the truck and you can have this cart to drive her to the pool. I'll take Summer to the barn."

Jamie scowled. Skyler showing up with the cart was too much of a coincidence. "Did Tommy say something?" Ellis would kill them both if he had. Jessica and Skyler were like second parents to them all, but Ellis was a very private person.

"Hold on, tiger. Let's get Jerry on his way and we'll talk a minute."

When they pulled up to the truck, Skyler slid out of the cart and strode over to the two women on the tailgate. After a quick hug for Jerry's mom and a peck on the lips for her wife, she had a quick, low conversation with Jessica.

Jessica nodded, hugged Jerry's mom good-bye, and headed for Ellis, who still held Summer's reins as the other two volunteers left for home. Ellis smiled, then looked over Jessica's shoulder at Jamie as Jessica began to talk. Crap. Ellis would be furious if she thought Jamie had ratted her out to Jessica and Skyler.

"Hey, a little help here," Skyler called, pulling Jamie's attention from the riding ring.

Jamie knew her role in the familiar routine. Jerry's wasted body wasn't all that heavy. She climbed into the truck on the driver's side so that when Skyler scooped Jerry up and lifted him into the doorway, Jamie pulled him into passenger seat and buckled him in.

"Thanks, ladies."

"Our pleasure," Skyler said.

"Later, dude." Jamie met his weak fist-bump and climbed out so Jerry's mom could get in to drive them home.

They watched the truck turn down the long drive, and Jamie rounded on Skyler.

"What's Jess talking to Ellis about, Skyler? If Tommy said anything, I'll kick his butt. She doesn't like people talking about her." Skyler's hand clamped on her shoulder stopped her tirade.

"James. Look at me." Skyler only used her pet name when she wanted to connect deep. "Tommy didn't say anything."

They were tight. Skyler had saved Jamie's family when she helped get her mom into an alcohol rehab program. She'd mentored Jamie as an amateur rider and promised the Parker Foundation would provide a college scholarship if Jamie wanted to pursue a degree in the equine industry. Their real bond, however, was their near-identical experiences as physically abused children. Jamie looked into Skyler's eyes and willed her, begged her to understand the disquiet that had been building in her for months, a turmoil that even she didn't understand.

"So, why'd you—"

"He only said he was going to bring Summer up for Ellis. The fact that she was in pain was written all over his face." Skyler paused and her voice softened. "Tommy's nursing a big crush on her. You know that, right?"

Jamie's chest tightened. "What? No. He's just a kid."

"He's grown four inches in the past year, and his voice cracks more than my granny's knees. He's not going to be a kid much longer, James."

The strange restlessness that'd haunted her for months swelled into a dark storm. "He better not touch her." She stiffened, startled by the growl in her voice, then glared at Skyler, daring her to challenge the declaration.

Skyler only cocked her head, the question in her eyes clear.

Jamie relented and dropped her gaze. She kicked petulantly at the dirt under her boot. "You know what I mean."

"Do *you*?"

The question hung in the air. Ellis was an affectionate friend. She frequently touched people as she talked and hugged when they met or parted. Was there more than that between them? Did Jamie want it to be more? She shrugged.

Skyler let it drop for now. "Anyway, Jess had already called my cell and told me she thought Ellis needed a ride from the ring." She smiled. "She knows Ellis pretty well, too, you know. She could see she's hurting some today."

Jamie glanced toward the ring. Ellis was watching Jamie, her expression worried, as Jessica continued to talk.

"So, why is she looking at me like that?"

"I might have exaggerated that little incident today when that horse pinned you against the wall of the trailer. Jess's telling Ellis what happened."

Jamie nearly growled. Why would Skyler intentionally make her look stupid in front of Ellis? That gelding was dumb as mud, but she should have anticipated he'd spook at nothing and suddenly swing his big butt around the wrong way. "Damn it, Sky. It was nothing. I'm fine."

Skyler continued as if Jamie hadn't spoken. "So Jess is explaining to Ellis that you're probably sore and could use some whirlpool therapy, but are too stubborn to admit that you're sore. Someone needs to persuade you to go up to the training center without making you feel like a big baby."

Jamie blinked at Skyler, then raised an eyebrow as realization dawned. "Exactly which part of me hurts?" She could almost feel Ellis watching and reached around to rub her lower back.

"Well, Jess is telling her it's your shoulder, but I guess you can say the pain has moved lower since you helped lift Jerry." She gave Jamie a speculative look. "But we'd better go get Ellis before any more of you falls apart."

Skyler indicated for Jamie to drive but turned to her as they settled in the cart. "If you need to talk about anything, sort out anything you're having trouble with, James, you know you can come to me, right? I was seventeen once, too, you know."

Jamie relaxed a little and bumped her shoulder against Skyler's. "Sure, Sky. I know."

❖

Jamie carefully feigned a small bit of stiffness when she exited the cart and smiled at Ellis. "Hey, Sky said she'll take Summer up to the barn and let me drive the cart. Want to ride with me?"

Since Summer was Ellis's responsibility as part of the therapy program, she looked to Jessica for permission.

"Go ahead." She looped her arm around Skyler's and entwined their fingers. The hub of the center was quiet, with most of the late-afternoon activity taking place in the barns or the paddocks behind them. "I'm not passing up this chance for a nice stroll with my wife. We'll put Summer in the wash line and turn her out for you."

Skyler stole a quick kiss. "Beat it, kids. And take the long way around. Adult time here," she said, never taking her eyes from Jessica's.

Ellis giggled, and Jamie huffed. "Whatever."

Then they all grinned as Ellis and Jamie climbed back into the cart.

❖

Skyler glanced back at the disappearing golf cart.

"Are you worried about them being in the pool without an adult there?" Jessica asked. "You know Jamie's a certified lifeguard."

"No. I'm worried about the three of them—Jamie, Ellis and Tommy—during the next year. It's a tough age. Jamie's been focused only on horses, but I think her dawn is breaking. Tommy, I'm afraid, is going to be an early bloomer. Ellis, I think, is there, but her shyness has held her back."

"Ah. You're talking about adolescent hormones."

Skyler chuckled. "Yeah. They're going to have to sort out some difficult things among themselves."

Jessica wrapped an arm around her wife. "You, Tory, and Marc survived jostling for girlfriends."

"Yes, but we weren't competing for each other. Tommy and Jamie, though I'm not sure she realizes it yet, are both crushing on Ellis. Somebody's going to get left out, or else they're both going to get their feelings hurt."

Jessica glanced away and Skyler recognized the familiar small smile. She knew something about this love triangle she wasn't revealing—likely Ellis's point of view. The only secrets they allowed between them were the confidences some of the kids trusted to each of them, as long as those secrets didn't endanger the welfare of the children or the program.

"It's hard to believe Jamie will start her senior year soon and leave us next year for college," Jessica said casually. "Ellis is on track to graduate early, but still a year behind her."

Skyler almost laughed. Her wife wasn't above hinting if the confidence was more like gossip and sure to be exposed soon anyway. "That's the other thing. Jamie hasn't settled on a college yet, and she needs to be thinking with her head, not her ovaries when she does. If she gets involved with Ellis now, I'm afraid she'll choose a school just because it's close to home."

They stopped when they reached the barn.

"It'll all be fine," Jessica said, tugging Skyler down for a quick kiss.

"You have a lot of faith in my Jamie."

"She has a great mentor." Jessica accepted a thank-you kiss. "And, I have a lot of faith in my Ellis."

❖

"Don't go tearing off like you usually do," Ellis warned her as Jamie slid into the driver's seat.

"I won't," Jamie said, pulling away slowly in the direction opposite of that taken by Skyler and Jessica, and carefully maneuvering around the few potholes in the well-maintained sandy driveway. Ellis braced against the gentle movement of the cart, her slim hand with bubblegum-pink painted nails splayed on the seat between them, and for a moment, Jamie imagined it possessively resting on her thigh instead. Jamie wasn't much of a talker and was used to Ellis chattering away when they were together. Today, she was unusually quiet. Too quiet.

"So, did you guys have a lot of clients today?"

"Five. No more than usual for a Saturday."

"You led all of them?"

"No." Ellis shot her an irritated look. "But I could if I wanted."

"I know. I just—" Okay. Maybe quiet was better than grumpy. "Never mind."

The equestrian center was designed like a wagon wheel, with the residence and riding arenas at the center and driveways leading outward like spokes to five barns and the training facility. The training facility, located on the north side of the center, housed an indoor pool, weight room, physical-therapy facilities, and a classroom where the young equestrians completed homework or were tutored. The turn leading to the training facility was next.

Ellis was probably pissed at her because she'd already figured out their con to get her up here. It wasn't her fault. It hadn't been her idea. So, should she wait for Ellis to say something? Hell no. She didn't care if Ellis bit her head off; she'd text Jessica to come back her up if Ellis refused. Ego be damned. She was going to get Ellis in that whirlpool even if she had to pick her up and carry her inside.

"Turn up there." Ellis barked the order before Jamie could slow the cart, and she obediently turned into the training facility's driveway. Neither of them moved to get out when she parked.

"Are you mad with me about something?" Jamie asked.

"Sky shouldn't have told you about—"

"I'm glad she did, because it's the only way I'd find out." Ellis's glare lasered into Jamie. "We're going in there and getting in that whirlpool and doing some stretches to work your soreness out. I don't want to hear any argument about it."

Oh. She wasn't mad about being conned. She still thought Jamie was actually injured. "You're the one who needs the water therapy, Ellis. You can't fool me. You didn't even fool Jerry. You could hardly walk out there."

The tears that filled Ellis's brown eyes sliced Jamie even deeper. "I feel like our relationship's one-sided, Jamie. You know when I'm hurting. But you never let me in. You never let me know when you're hurting. You never let me take care of you."

Jamie blinked. She opened her mouth but couldn't find words. Blindsided. Sucker-punched. Panic filled her. She gathered Ellis's hand in hers and stared at it, unable to hold her gaze. "My back isn't hurt. I promise. Jess and Sky told you that so you'd come with me and get in the whirlpool." Her throat closed, and it took a moment to work out the next words. They were talking about more than Ellis's leg and Jamie's back. She wasn't ready, but this was Ellis. This was important. "But hearing that you feel like I don't need you does hurt me." Her last words were hardly more than a whisper.

She looked up to meet Ellis's gaze, and, still holding tight to her hand, Jamie reached with her other hand to brush away Ellis's tears. Her skin was so smooth, so warm. The gesture felt intimate, like more than friendship. A softness lit Ellis's eyes and warmed Jamie. Her fear receded a little. Things were changing between them. "Let's go inside, okay? We'll talk, I promise."

Ellis silently accepted Jamie's help, draping her arm over Jamie's shoulder while Jamie wrapped her arm securely around Ellis's waist so she bore most of her weight as she hobbled into the training facility. They retrieved swimsuits from their lockers. Most of the girls changed in the open locker room, but several curtained dressing rooms were available for the few who were shy. Since they were senior among the girls, nobody ever questioned why Ellis and Jamie always changed in the private rooms.

Jamie helped Ellis onto the bench in one changing room, then hesitated. "Can you manage okay?" Ellis flushed red, and Jamie willed her mind not to speculate the reason.

"Can you pull off my boots for me?"

"Sure." Jamie knelt and pulled the left knee-length boot free. She felt Ellis tense when she took hold of the right. "I'll be careful." This boot was much harder to remove, and Ellis gave a small cry when her heel slipped free and her foot extended to slip through the shank of the boot. "Damn, Ellis." Her ankle was very swollen. "We need to ice this."

"Heat first, then ice," Ellis said through her clenched teeth. She took a deep breath and offered a weak smile. "You go get changed. I can handle the rest here."

Jamie backed away. "Okay. Get your suit on, but don't go anywhere. I'll be right outside when you're ready. Just holler."

Ellis nodded and motioned for Jamie to pull the curtain closed. She raced to the next stall, stripped, and dressed quickly in her swimsuit. She picked up the short-sleeved surfer rashguard she always wore over it but didn't put it on.

"Ready when you are," Ellis said quietly.

Jamie pulled the curtain back. Ellis sucked in a breath and stared.

"Holy crap, Jamie."

Jamie shifted her feet uncertainly. She wasn't sure what to say. This was a bad idea. She started to put her shirt on over the two-piece suit.

"Don't. I mean." Ellis swallowed. "You're gorgeous. I don't know why you always wear that rashguard over your suit. I sure wouldn't if I had your body."

Jamie hugged the shirt to her chest as if it could protect her even as she prepared to bare herself to Ellis. "I wear it to hide something, Ellis. I need to show you. I need you to understand."

She sat on the bench next to Ellis and turned slowly to reveal her back. Jamie tried not to flinch at Ellis's gasp. She closed her eyes at the feather-light touch of Ellis's fingertips on the old scars that marred her back. "I was just a little kid when I learned to hide that I hurt." She turned back to Ellis. "I don't mean to shut you out. I just don't know how to let people in. Skyler's working with me on that. But even she has to call me on it sometimes and make me open up." She reached for Ellis's hand. "I'm not ready to take the shirt off around anyone else, but if you feel like I'm shutting you out, just tell me. I can be kind of thickheaded sometimes. Make me talk to you, okay?"

Ellis squeezed her hand. "Okay. I promise."

"But you have to tell me when your leg is hurting, too, and stop being stubborn about letting me and Tommy help you."

Ellis dropped her eyes to their joined hands. "I'm not sure I can walk out to the pool since we took my boot off."

Jamie stood, then bent to slide one arm behind Ellis's back and the other behind her knees. "Put your arms around my neck and hold on tight."

"Jamie!" Ellis squealed when Jamie easily hefted her from the bench. "You're going to hurt—"

"My back isn't hurt, remember?" Jamie had been training as an amateur equestrian since she was eleven years old. She was four inches taller and nearly thirty pounds of muscle heavier than Ellis. "You're light as a feather."

Ellis laughed. "My hero."

She felt like a superhero when Ellis relaxed and rested her head against Jamie's shoulder. Ellis's two-piece suit was a modest racer style, but everywhere their skin touched distracted Jamie, so she had to concentrate to step carefully through the locker room and into the area that housed the pool and a large hot tub. Knowing the steps into the hot tub could be slippery, she stood

Ellis on the pool's edge, then climbed down to place her hands on Ellis's waist to help her into the warm water.

Jamie braced to take Ellis's weight but didn't anticipate the water jets would activate and knock her off balance at the same moment. She clutched Ellis to her as they slipped under the water while she scrambled to find footing. The seconds until they emerged, sputtering, seemed like an eternity. Her heart was pounding, but Ellis was laughing.

Then Ellis stopped laughing and tightened her arms around Jamie's shoulders. The whir of the water jets was making Jamie dizzy. Or was it Ellis's bare belly slick against hers because Jamie held her just as tight? They were nose-to-nose, Ellis's breasts pressed against hers. She should let go. But Ellis hadn't. Her heart pounded faster. She couldn't catch her breath. God, she was going to hyperventilate. There. The light. That softness she'd seen before in Ellis's eyes. She soaked it up and closed her eyes to hold it in.

Then the softness found her lips. Ellis. So warm. A taste, she needed just a taste. Jamie flicked her tongue out and Ellis hummed her consent, opening and meeting Jamie's probe. So sweet. Ellis's favorite butterscotch candy. Her head buzzed and every cell of her body tingled. Ellis, oh, Ellis. She was a field of green clover. She was the scent of fresh-cut hay. She was the ice cream on hot apple pie. She was better than the best of everything, anything Jamie had ever experienced.

A door slammed in another part of the facility, and Jamie gently disengaged. Ellis still held on to her shoulders, not letting her go far. They stared shyly at each other.

Jamie was afraid she'd wake up at any moment and find the kiss had been only a dream. She'd known for a while that she was same-sex oriented. She'd also realized her feelings for Ellis were more than friendship. But she was practiced at hiding her feelings and determined to never let Ellis know. Unless Ellis indicated *she* wanted more than friendship. Maybe Ellis was just curious and not really serious. She searched Ellis's eyes. If ever she needed truth, if ever she needed tough love, it was now. "What are you thinking?"

"University of New Hampshire."

Jamie's heart sank. Obviously, they weren't on the same page. She was thinking that they were alone, nearly naked in each other's arms. She was imagining Ellis without her swim top. She was thinking of a second kiss. She looked away and loosened her hold on Ellis. "Okay."

Ellis tightened her hold, giving Jamie a little shake. "I think you should apply to the University of New Hampshire. Jessica says they have a first-class eventing program and a four-year degree in equestrian studies that has three possible tracks. You can go for the industry-and-business-management track or the science track for pre-vet students. It's perfect for you."

"It's a long way from Virginia." Jamie looked into Ellis's eyes again. A quick cut is better than a slow drowning. She steeled herself. "Are you trying to get rid of me?"

Ellis jerked back in surprise. "Was my kiss that bad?"

"I wasn't the one thinking of colleges while we were kissing."

Ellis slid close again, hooking her good leg around Jamie's hips. "I wasn't thinking of colleges while we were kissing. I was thinking that you're the best kisser ever."

Jamie relaxed a little. "You've kissed other people?"

"Well, no. But I'm sure if I had, you'd be the best."

"Yeah?" Jamie cupped Ellie's hips to hold her above the water as she sank to their shoulders so that the edge of the hot tub hid them from immediate view of whoever was slamming doors in the locker-room area.

"Definitely."

"So, what's up with the college talk?"

"The third track they offer is therapeutic riding." Ellis dropped her gaze to Jamie's mouth, tracing her fingertip over Jamie's lips. "So, I was planning to apply to go there when I graduate the next year."

"Really?"

"Yeah." Ellis raised her eyes to Jamie's, her expression uncertain. "If I wouldn't be crowding you."

Crowding her? The water jets paused, and in the ensuing quiet, Jamie realized the storm that had been building inside her for the past year had calmed. The jagged pieces of her life were falling into place. There would still be bumps. Tommy still had a crush on Ellis, and neither of them wanted to hurt him. She still had to get through her senior year of high school and navigate this new thing between her and Ellis.

"So, what are you thinking?"

The tentative quiver in Ellis's voice jerked her back to the present. Jamie smiled and gazed into eyes the color of dark, warm honey.

"I was thinking New Hampshire is a great idea." She moved closer, her lips nearly touching Ellis's. "Especially if it includes kissing. Lots of kissing."

And so they sealed their new plan with a second kiss.

Jamie is a character who appeared briefly in D. Jackson Leigh's Bareback. *This story evolved from several readers' requests for more about her.*

PASSION'S BOND

Haze

"Where are you?"

"Home. In Maryland." I'd expected the call from Dante. My cousin was the brother my parents hadn't given me, and I was supposed to be on the West Coast at his oceanside estate when he returned from vacationing in Europe. "Don't worry. Tom's still in a cast, but he's getting around well enough to supervise a helper, and I paid for the extra help since I didn't stay like I promised."

Dante sighed heavily. Drama was his forte and life was his stage. "You didn't have to do that, but you do have to tell me why you needed to go home early. Is something wrong?"

Everything was wrong.

I knew if I woke you I wouldn't be strong enough to leave, so I'll let last night's kisses be our good-bye.

"Haze?" His voice carried true concern.

"Nothing. Nothing's wrong." I hated lying to him. "The media circus has shifted to the latest celebrity death by overdose, so I thought it was safe to come home. Your place is great, but I can't hide forever."

"Uh-huh. Are you sure your early exit didn't have something to do with my sexy neighbor?"

"I don't know what you're talking about." My pain was too fresh. I was too wounded to share it.

"That's all anyone is talking about around town."

"I thought you said people around there know how to keep their mouths shut."

He huffed. "They don't talk to outsiders, but Matt and I are hardly outsiders."

I couldn't stop myself. "Have you seen her?"

"No, but I saw Juan Carlos in town. He said she's been painting nonstop all day and riding the beach half the night since she returned. What went on between you two?"

I was the white linen she loved to wear—stained now, so she threw me away. She would get new. I couldn't tell him that, but I knew he wouldn't stop hounding me until I confessed something.

"We enjoyed each other for a short while. That's all." Then I threw him a different bone to chase. "You know the awards thing is next week. I've decided to go."

"Oh, sweetie. Really?"

"Since I'm one of the honorees, I think not going would just make me look guilty of something I'm not."

"Do you need an escort? I can fly over for the weekend."

In spite of everything, I smiled at his offer. He'd just spent four months traveling and had to be road weary.

"I need to face this music alone, but be prepared to pack an overnight bag and head for the airport in case I lose my nerve."

"Say the word and I'm there."

I knew he meant it. I could always count on Dante. I couldn't say the same for him counting on me. Hadn't I tucked my tail and run before he returned home? Just like I'd run to him when my life fell apart here? I hated that I was such a coward. Would things have been different if I'd found the courage to tell Luna what I felt for her? I rubbed the ache in my chest as if it were a physical pain. How could she not know? I'd told her in a thousand different ways in the poems I penned.

"Thanks. I…I'll be okay." I silently cursed the break in my voice.

"I'm going to call you next week before the gala," he said

after a moment. "And, if you screen your calls and don't answer, I'll be on the first plane out there." His tone held a gentle warning, and I loved him for it.

I brought our conversation to a close before I lost my composure. Not even Dante had seen me so emotionally naked. Only Maddie, my best friend since college, knew the Haze who cried when she penned mournful verse, who had wanted to be a rock star instead of a poet, and who needed to be held and consoled after her old dog was euthanized. That paparazzi photo had taken her from me. We were in the Rose Garden and I sobbed in her arms. Her gentle, consoling kiss was but a brush of her lips against mine. But political enemies used it to manufacture a false affair to embarrass Maddie's husband, the President of the United States.

My anger had been a constant companion as I fled the media storm and took refuge at Ravencroft. I had no anger to keep me company now. Only a vast, empty ache where Luna had been.

"She'll tear your heart out."

"Pardon?" I'd been studying the painting I'd seen on my first visit to the gallery—the naked woman sitting in the window, a smoldering cigarette dangling from her fingers—and turned to find that very woman staring at me. "Did you say something?"

She jerked her chin toward the painting. "When she's captured you on canvas to her satisfaction, then she'll be done with you."

I wasn't sure if I saw pain or pity in her eyes, and when I hesitated, she took it as encouragement to say more, her voice low and bitter.

"She's fucking your brains out right now and sketching you every minute. Am I right?"

I stared at her. My mouth, my brain, my emotions were frozen with false denial.

"Yeah. I thought so." She looked back at the painting. "Been there, done that."

My lip twitched, but I held back the snarl that begged to surface. I'd give her nothing. "I have no idea what you're talking about."

She made a disgusted sound and glanced back toward the stairs where we could hear Luna and Angelo descending from the loft. She put her face inches from mine and whispered through gritted teeth. "Remember what I said. When she finishes your portrait, she's done with you."

They made their way to us—Luna's expression wary and Angelo's gleeful at finding the two of us talking.

"Hello, Jackie." Luna hardly glanced at her and completely ignored me. She pointed to a seascape hanging on the wall. "That one," she said to Angelo as she scanned the rest hanging on the back wall. She pointed to the portrait of Jackie as if the woman in the painting were a stranger, as if Jackie weren't standing right there. "And that one. It should sell easily in New York."

"No!" Jackie jumped forward and took it from the wall. "I want to buy it."

I took a step back, recoiling as though her wound had opened and her dignity was bleeding onto the floor, like she had vomited her desperation at our feet.

"If you want it, it's yours. A gift." Luna's response held no pity, but no kindness either. Her neutral tone invited Jackie to regain her composure but ignored her pain. I was uncertain if I should feel concerned or ambivalent.

Jackie's face hardened, and I was relieved that she seemed to be stuffing her desolation back into her wound and holding it closed again. "I don't want charity." She turned to Angelo. "How much?"

Luna held up her hand to forestall Angelo's reply. "Five hundred for Angelo's commission."

My mind raced back to the "Night Watcher" painting sold to me. It seemed the man made a fine living from Luna's trysts. The thought choked me. Was I just another tryst?

"If you won't accept it as a gift, then consider it payment for posing as my model," Luna said.

Jackie glared, her throat working. "Then I was just a high-priced whore to you?"

The remark was cruel, and Luna appeared to realize it as soon as the words left her lips. Her expression softened into something like resignation. "No. You were a friend, but you wanted more and I didn't, I don't." She held Jackie's gaze. "Please take the painting, Jackie. A memento, not a payment." She pointed out a different painting to Angelo. "Send that one to New York."

"The seascape to Philadelphia then?"

"Yes."

He gently took the painting from Jackie. "Should I wrap this for you?"

Jackie looked to me as though I might have the answer. I had none to give her, so she turned back to Angelo. "Can you box it? I'm packing up and heading back to San Francisco." I heard decision, not rancor in her voice, and she followed Angelo without sparing Luna another glance or a good-bye.

Despite Jackie's warning that I would be burned, I'd walked willingly into Luna's fire. Now, I was home and licking my wounds. Actually, I wasn't even doing that. None of the things jilted people do—indulging in comfort food, shopping extravagantly, drinking themselves into a stupor—held any appeal.

I read somewhere that depressed people sleep a lot, but I could only lie in bed and stare at the ceiling. Every time I closed my eyes, my mind conjured what I'd seen when I opened them the morning Luna had left me—the dreaded painting Jackie had warned me about.

She'd captured me sitting in the sun in my usual boy-shorts. My ever-present notebook was resting on the arm of my lounger, my pen poised above it as I paused and gazed at the artist over the top of my sunglasses. She'd exercised artistic license in painting my eyes a lush forest green. When I look in the mirror now, they're a flat, murky pond. I left it there, along with her kiss-off note.

I knew if I woke you I wouldn't be strong enough to leave, so I'll let last night's kisses be our good-bye.

Did she leave all her lovers with just a note? I wasn't a loser like Jackie. I wouldn't accept Luna's consolation gift. Instead, I left a gift of my own. A note next to hers.

The moon is but an interlude,
a lovely dance of dream.

A dark beauty, she's bejeweled with stars.
Still, her magic does wax, then wane.

For the moon is but an interlude,
'til day again will reign.

Give the painting to Angelo. I don't think I'm being arrogant to suggest he could turn it for a very handsome profit, considering my reputation as the first lady's lesbian lover.

It was cold, but it was better than my first impulse to slash the portrait into ribbons, the way she'd sliced me into bitter bits. The words had spilled from my pen like blood from a beheading, but I hadn't written a single verse since. Weren't writers supposed to turn their worst moments into their best work?

Every brooding hour sank me lower into my abyss, and it was time to grab a bootstrap. I was stomping my feet into my riding boots when my cell rang. The caller's ID was blocked, so I didn't answer it. I was weary of games and refused to talk to anyone hiding behind "unidentified caller."

I cast around the mudroom for where I'd left my riding gloves and spotted them under the deacon's bench. I was kneeling to retrieve them when my phone chimed to signal a voice mail. I ignored it. It was probably some reporter who'd just realized my name was still on the list for the Medal of Freedom Awards. I grabbed my gloves and had my hand on the doorknob. Damn it. I shouldn't ride alone without taking my phone. Once it was in my hand, I couldn't resist punching the speed dial for voice mail.

I'm hoping this went to voice mail because you're screening your calls and not because you've gone riding without your cell again. Please, please call me back at this number right away.

I couldn't dial fast enough. "Maddie?"

"Haze. God, it's good to hear your voice." Hers was a beacon piercing my dark mood.

"Are you in D.C.?"

"Where else? I'm still serving time in this prison they call The White House. I'm using a friend's phone." Long pause, then a sniff. "I was afraid you wouldn't answer if you saw my number on your caller ID."

The tears at the edge of her voice tore at me. "I'll always answer when you call. Screw the fuckers and their politics."

"That's the Haze I know and love." She sighed. "I miss you terribly."

"I'll see you at the awards thing next weekend."

"Really? Oh, thank you, Jesus."

"Unless I've been elevated to deity, I don't think Jesus has anything to do with it." Maddie was a Southerner, and I loved to tease her about her colloquial verbiage. I smiled at the floor when she laughed. I so needed her right now.

"I heard a rumor that you can walk on water."

"It's true. Every winter when the pond freezes over." I could picture her shaking her head now.

"It's a good thing you can write poetry because you couldn't make a living writing jokes." Her admonishment was full of affection. "So, I should put your RSVP down as Baird and guest?"

"No guest. Dante just got back from Europe, and it's too much to ask for him to fly across country again so soon."

"I wasn't thinking of Dante." Her tone was teasing.

"You finally got a number for that private escort service rumored to cater to Capitol Hill?" It was an old joke between us.

"What? No. I just thought…I met your artist at a gallery opening here a few weeks ago."

Maddie had met Luna? I slumped onto the hard bench, sucked instantly back into my quagmire of misery. "She's not my artist."

"But—"

"Not anymore." My throat tightened. "I can't…I don't want to talk about it."

"Haze. What did you do?"

Why was everything always my fault? Why was I the one who supposedly seduced the president's wife? Why would I be the cause of my split with Luna?

"She dumped me, okay?" I choked on the truth of it and had to draw a deep breath before I could speak again. "That's all I'm going to say."

I was tempted to end the call during the long silence that followed.

"You're really in love with her." Maddie sounded surprised.

I didn't answer.

"Oh, honey. There must be some misunderstanding—"

"Drop it, Maddie, or I'm going to hang up right now."

"Okay, okay, geez."

Her sophomoric whine propelled me back to our college dorm. Her probing, me deflecting. We'd done this dance for nearly twenty years since we were freshies, and she knew if she let me stew I'd eventually boil over and spill it. I loved her persistence. Without it, I wouldn't have published my first poem or my first book. I never would have won a Pulitzer or been named the United States Poet Laureate.

I could hear an intercom in the background. "Where are you?"

"Visiting a friend in the hospital."

"Nothing serious, I hope."

She sighed. "The partner of my chief secret-service agent is a doctor here. I'm in her office, because she was kind enough to let me use her cell phone. She's not a public figure, so the media can't demand her phone records."

"Smart."

"It pisses me off that I can't even call my best friend for a private chat."

"Will John run for reelection?"

"Only if he wants a divorce. I'm not doing this again. He promised me one term, then children."

"You're finally going to make me an aunt?" I was happy to turn the attention back to her.

"If he gets out of politics and goes back to teaching it instead. I want less stress in our lives. I want a picket fence and a minivan and kids I have to drive to soccer practice. I hate politics. Especially since it's come between us." Someone was speaking to her. "Haze, I have to go. The good doctor needs her office back, and if I stay any longer the media will be speculating that I'm getting breast implants or have some dreadful disease."

"Okay." I wanted just another few seconds with her. "Maddie?"

"Yes?"

"Thanks for calling."

"Promise you won't back out of the awards?" She knew me too well. My vow would mean more than making her happy. It would keep me from agonizing over the decision, because only an act of God could make me break my word to her.

"I promise."

❖

I checked myself in the mirror one more time. The royal-blue brocade of the tailored jacket, the plunging neckline of the collarless black silk blouse, and the flare of my low-cut pants gave a feminine twist to my tuxedo. I wasn't a stickler for brands, but Armani understood women who needed to look regal rather than girly. At least I was satisfied with the design. Nothing on this planet could get me in a dress, but I wasn't comfortable in a man's tux either.

I was nervous. Last night, I'd prayed for the flu, a mysterious fever, appendicitis—anything that could justify my absence. Alas. I'd awakened that morning, hale and hearty except for a bit of nausea from nerves.

Six of us were receiving Presidential Medal of Freedom Awards. I was the first poet since Maya Angelou, and I felt totally underqualified for the honor when compared to her.

The evening was carefully staged, a complete waste of good tax dollars. All the recipients, even the one who lived in the D.C. area, were put up for the weekend in suites at the Four Seasons. Six limousines picked us up at fifteen-minute intervals so we arrived individually to walk past the media and gawkers and into The Kennedy Center.

I was glad I wasn't first but felt ridiculous alone in a stretch limo that could have held fifteen people. The day had been a whirlwind of interviews and television appearances, leaving me little time for private thoughts. But alone in my luxurious transport, I tortured myself with a fantasy of Luna sitting next to me, our fingers entwined, resting on my thigh. I would have poured champagne for us to sip. She would have stroked my cheek to calm my nerves. She would have kissed me, then laughed and wiped her gloss from my lips.

But she wasn't here, and I stared forlornly as Washington

moved past outside my tinted windows. The night couldn't be over too soon for me. I only hoped I would catch a glimpse, maybe even a moment with Maddie. It would be hard, I knew, among the pomp and circumstance and prowling media. I was already calculating how soon I could sneak out of the reception and dance that would follow the awards ceremony.

I should have taken Dante up on his offer. At least we could have passed the time dancing. I gave in when, as teens, he begged me to partner with him for a ballroom-dancing class. It was fun, and we turned out to be very good students. I wished him here now, being dramatic, making jokes about women's dresses, drooling over their handsome escorts.

My morose thoughts followed like black clouds as I stepped out of the limo to a barrage of camera flashes and shouts.

"Miss Baird, over here."

"Haze, will you dance with the first lady tonight?"

"Have you talked to the first lady?"

"Are you here alone?"

"Is it true you've been hiding out in Europe these past few months?"

"Has the president spoken with you, Ms. Baird?"

"Are you wearing Armani?"

I stopped and looked for the source of the last question. The slight, fair-haired guy was easily recognizable from one of those television fashion shows, and I smiled at him. There's a reason we refer to our LGBT community as family. I looked into his clear blue eyes and saw Dante and every other gay brother or lesbian sister. I wasn't as alone as I'd thought. "Yes. I am," I said.

The crowd fell silent, straining to hear if I'd answer any of the other questions.

I winked at him. "My boots are Alexander Wang, and my underwear is from Victoria's Secret."

"Awesome," he said, grinning.

The pandemonium erupted again when I resumed my red-carpet walk, my back a little straighter, my head held a little higher for the first time since boarding the plane in California to come home.

❖

I shifted nervously in the wings, my moment near at hand. I was mid-pack in the limo lineup, but dead last to receive my award.

We all sat in the front row of a box where everyone could see us, and I waited restlessly as each was tapped on the shoulder to descend and wait in the wings while the lights dimmed and video rolled of their accomplishments. When the stage lights came up again, the President of the United States would be standing at the podium and the honoree walked across the stage to stand while John added a few scripted words about their worthiness, then handed over their medal.

My video footage was playing now. Fifteen years younger, I was reading from *Same but Different*, the collection of poems that had launched my career. Then I was helping college students, children in the projects of Atlanta, and Cherokee elders find their poetic voice. I was speaking before the United Nations on behalf of the LGBT community worldwide. Then I was accepting the Pulitzer for *You Don't See Me*.

When the lights began to come up, I stared at the floor for a few seconds to adjust to the brightness. Then I took a deep breath, praying I didn't trip and that John would be brief. I hadn't taken a full step when the stage manager grabbed my arm and held me back.

"Not yet," he whispered.

I looked at him in confusion, then followed his nod to the podium. Maddie stood in John's place. I could see only the stubborn set of her profile, her chin thrust out; but on the monitor beside me, her eyes blazed as she stared down the audience until their murmurs quieted. My image was frozen on the huge screen behind her, and she turned to look at me, then back to the audience.

"The first time I saw Haze Baird, we were both freshmen at Cambridge. She was standing between a bloodied young Asian student and three brawny frat boys. She was one against three and no one else was stepping up to help, so I joined her to even the odds, and the cowardly bullies left for easier prey."

At last, she turned to me, eyes shining, and held out her hand. A gentle push from the stage manager sent me across the stage, and I was surprised when I took her damp hand in mine. I would have never guessed she was nervous. She drew me alongside her and addressed the crowd again.

"I asked John to break with protocol and let me present this award because Haze has been my champion every day since I joined her to defend our fellow student. She tutored me through English class, talked me into going on a blind date with the man who later became my husband"—she gave me a sideways glance—"and she has taken his side in most of our disagreements." She paused while I smiled and shook my head. "She was my maid of honor at our wedding, although my mother will never forgive her for wearing a tux instead of a dress."

She waited until the chuckles quieted and every ear was listening for her next words. "Our friendship is a deep bond because I've never known Haze Baird to do a single cowardly, disloyal, unethical, or disrespectful thing. I can't say the same for some media and politicians." Sound byte. News at eleven.

She took the medal from its box. "On behalf of the President of the United States, I award you this Medal of Freedom in recognition of your efforts to champion the cause of millions who are slighted because of their race, ethnic background, gender, or sexual orientation."

I bent down so she could fasten its wide ribbon around my neck.

"Surprised?" she whispered as she worked the catch.

"Shocked," I murmured back.

"Now that I've said all those wonderful things about you, don't be a coward, Haze, and everything will be okay." She kissed my cheek and returned to her seat. I blinked, wondering if I'd misunderstood her words because of the loud applause.

John stood and shook my hand, then pulled me into a brief hug. That photo would make a few front pages. The rest was a blur—the other medal recipients joining me onstage, a patriotic musical finale, a photo session, and lots of hand-shaking. Maddie had disappeared, and, when I asked about her, John smiled and shrugged. "You know Maddie. She's always up to something."

❖

A vase of bloodred roses greeted me when I returned to my dressing room. The card propped against it quoted my own work.

I would die a thousands deaths before I would live a single second without passion. It is the fuel of ambition, the compost that grows everything good.

It is the bond that seals love.

Don't be a coward, Haze. Take a chance on passion's bond.

Maddie

There it was again. What did she mean by that? I was too exhausted to decipher it.

The room was blissfully empty and quiet. I was the only female recipient and thankfully didn't have to share my space. Even though seeing Maddie did lift my spirits, I'm basically a quiet, solitary person. Being around a crowd drains me, and after a month of sulking over Luna, I was all out of reserves.

I had an hour before I had to join the reception line in the ballroom, and I intended to spend it in the dark, prone on my dressing-room couch, plotting my early escape from tonight's honoree ball. First I wanted to get clean of this dreadful second skin of television makeup. I spurned the cold cream at the makeup desk and went straight for soap and water in the adjoining bathroom. I scrubbed my face, toweled it dry, and straightened to check for missed spots. That's when I saw it taped to the mirror.

The moon is but an interlude,
a lovely dance of dreams.

A dark beauty, she's bejeweled with stars.
Still, her magic does wax, then wane.

For the moon is but an interlude,
'til day again will reign.

Give the painting to Angelo. I don't think I'm being arrogant to suggest he could turn it for a very handsome profit, considering my reputation as the first lady's lesbian lover.

"Maddie says there's been a terrible misunderstanding."

I spun around, instantly gripped in a visceral quickening of my traitorous libido. Luna was more beautiful than my most vivid memory. Her hair was caught up in a French twist, wheat-colored strands strategically loose in a casually elegant style that left the clean, tantalizing lines of her shoulders bare. My mouth watered, my lips twitched to taste the caramel skin above her glittering white strapless evening dress.

"I'm not great with words, Haze, but your message seemed pretty clear to me. Did I misinterpret it?"

I swallowed and forced my eyes to her. The edge in her

words, the hurt in her eyes didn't belong to my carefree Luna. I hung my head. "No. You didn't."

We stood there for a long moment, her watching me, me gripping the towel still in my hands and studying the floor.

"It was so very cold, and I had thought you were my sun."

Her quiet resignation confused me. Why would she expect me to react differently? The rustle of her dress as she moved to walk out of my dressing room, of my life, put flame to my frozen brain.

"What did you expect? You couldn't even end us in person."

She whirled on me. This was my Luna, passionate and so furious that I wanted to step back. I wanted to run to her. I hovered in indecision as she loosed a verbal assault, unfortunately too rapid for my rudimentary Spanish. I did catch enough to understand some impressively creative cursing.

I scowled. "I can't understand you."

She closed the distance between us and poked me in the chest to punctuate her words. "I don't understand *you*. I worked for weeks on that painting for you. It is my very best work."

"It was a consolation prize. I'm not Jackie."

She stepped back, and another string of Spanish curses filled the small room before she switched to English. "What in the hell does Jackie have to do with this?"

"I wasn't going to let you send me away with a painting as payment for my services."

Luna stared at me, her lips parted, but no words came out.

The pot Maddie had been waiting to boil finally spilled over. "She tried to warn me that day in the gallery. She said that when you finished my painting, you'd be finished with me. Just like you'd finished with her."

"I fucked Jackie once." She waved her hand dismissively. "Maybe two or three times. I—" Her eyes filled and she twisted away so I could no longer see her face. "I *shared* myself with you."

My confusion deepened. "Then why'd you leave me?"

She threw her arms up in an exasperated gesture and faced me again. Tears wet her cheeks, but her voice was strong. "You have to do readings and lectures. I must cater to gallery owners so they will show my paintings." Her voice softened. "I was coming back."

I wasn't ready to give up my high ground. "You left me a consolation painting and a kiss-off note. 'I'll let last night's kisses be our good-bye.'"

She smacked my shoulder, her voice rising. "Until I came back."

I matched her volume. "You didn't say that."

We each glared at the other, arms crossed over our chests. It was a senseless standoff. We apparently wanted the same thing. I rubbed my shoulder where she'd whacked me. "You hurt me."

She made an impatient sound, but the tense set of her shoulders relaxed. "You're a big, impulsive baby. Juan Carlos was waiting to take me to the airport. If I'd woke you, you would have looked at me with those make-love-to-me eyes, and then we'd have been naked again and I'd have missed my plane."

"That's not what your note conveyed."

"Maybe I'm not good with words, but you read into them what you expected me to say." Her eyes reflected the same hurt that had gnawed me for weeks. "You didn't trust my feelings for you."

"You never told me how you felt." I sounded like an impudent child.

"And you never told me what *you* were feeling." She sighed. "I left you a portrait, a picture of my passion reflected in your eyes, and you left me a 'get-lost' poem."

When she put it that way, it did sound harsh.

I stared at the floor and shrugged. "So, I'm not good at interpreting art."

I could bravely bare myself to millions in pages of

poetic verse, but admitting my heart to this beautiful woman immobilized me...*don't be a coward, Haze, and everything will be okay.* "I love you," I whispered.

A few seconds of silence. "Are you saying that to the floor or to me?"

I looked up and found her gaze. "I love you, Luna. The first time I saw you on the beach, my heart called for you because it beats only when yours does."

I was a master of pretty words, so her eyes searched mine for sincerity. I grabbed Maddie's card and fell to my knees as I offered it to her. Her eyes filled as she read it, then held it to her heart. I took her hand in mine. "Don't be a coward, Luna."

"I love you, too," she choked out. She took a steadying breath. "Tell me what you want."

I looked up at her. "I want to write a thousand sonnets, all about you."

She smiled. "I want to fill the house with your image so I'll never be alone."

"I want to ride the beach together, every night under the moonlight." I stood but kept her hand in mine. "I want to wake up with you in my arms every morning."

Her hand was warm against my cheek, then firm as it cupped my nape. "I want you to kiss me."

I drew her to me and gave her my lips as I'd given her my heart. I was her sun and she my moon, forever bound by our dance of passion.

About the Author

D. Jackson Leigh grew up barefoot and happy, swimming in farm ponds and riding rude ponies in rural south Georgia. Her passion for writing led her to a career in journalism and North Carolina, where she edits breaking news at night and writes lesbian romance stories with equestrian settings by day.

She was awarded a 2010 Alice B. Lavender Certificate for Noteworthy Accomplishment and was a finalist in the 2013 LGBT Rainbow Awards for erotic romance and in the 2014 Lambda Literary Awards romance category. She is the winner of a 2013 Golden Crown Literary Society Award in the paranormal romance category for *Touch Me Gently* and a 2014 GCLS Award in the romance category for *Every Second Counts*.

Visit her at djacksonleigh.com or friend her on Facebook (D Jackson Leigh) or Twitter (@djacksonleigh).

Books Available From Bold Strokes Books

The 45th Parallel by Lisa Girolami. Burying her mother isn't the worst thing that can happen to Val Montague when she returns to the woodsy but peculiar town of Hemlock, Oregon. (978-1-62639-342-4)

A Royal Romance by Jenny Frame. In a country where class still divides, can love topple the last social taboo and allow Queen Georgina and Beatrice Elliot, a working-class girl, their happy ever after? (978-1-62639-360-8)

Bouncing by Jaime Maddox. Basketball coach Alex Dalton has been bouncing from woman to woman because no one ever held her interest, until she meets her new assistant, Britain Dodge. (978-1-62639-344-8)

Same Time Next Week by Emily Smith. A chance encounter between Alex Harris and the beautiful Michelle Masters leads to a whirlwind friendship and causes Alex to question everything she's ever known—including her own marriage. (978-1-62639-345-5)

All Things Rise by Missouri Vaun. Cole rescues a striking pilot who crash-lands near her family's farm, setting in motion a chain of events that will forever alter the course of her life. (978-1-62639-346-2)

Riding Passion by D. Jackson Leigh. Mount up for the ride through a sizzling anthology of chance encounters, buried desires, romantic surprises, and blazing passion. (978-1-62639-349-3)

Love's Bounty by Yolanda Wallace. Lobster boat captain Jake Myers stopped living the day she cheated death, but meeting greenhorn Shy Silva stirs her back to life. (978-1-62639334-9)

Just Three Words by Melissa Brayden. Sometimes the one you want is the one you least suspect…Accountant Samantha Ennis has her ordered life disrupted when heartbreaker Hunter Blair moves into her trendy Soho loft. (978-1-62639-335-6)

Lay Down the Law by Carsen Taite. Attorney Peyton Davis returns to her Texas roots to take on big oil and the Mexican Mafia, but will her investigation thwart her chance at true love? (978-1-62639-336-3)

Playing in Shadow by Lesley Davis. Survivor's guilt threatens to keep Bryce trapped in her nightmare world unless Scarlet's love can pull her out of the darkness back into the light. (978-1-62639-337-0)

Soul Selecta by Gill McKnight. Soul mates are hell to work with. (978-1-62639-338-7)

The Revelation of Beatrice Darby by Jean Copeland. Adolescence is complicated, but Beatrice Darby is about to discover how impossible it can seem to a lesbian coming of age in conservative 1950s New England. (978-1-62639-339-4)

Twice Lucky by Mardi Alexander. For firefighter Mackenzie James and Dr. Sarah Mackenzie, there's suddenly a whole lot more in life to understand, to consider, to risk…someone will need to fight for her life. (978-1-62639-325-7)

Shadow Hunt by L.L. Raand. With young to raise and her Pack under attack, Sylvan, Alpha of the wolf Weres, takes on her greatest challenge when she determines to uncover the faceless enemies known as the Shadow Lords. A Midnight Hunters novel. (978-1-62639-326-4)

Heart of the Game by Rachel Spangler. A baseball writer falls for a single mom, but can she ever love anything as much as she loves the game? (978-1-62639-327-1)

Getting Lost by Michelle Grubb. Twenty-eight days, thirteen European countries, a tour manager fighting attraction, and an accused murderer: Stella and Phoebe's journey of a lifetime begins here. (978-1-62639-328-8)

Prayer of the Handmaiden by Merry Shannon. Celibate priestess Kadrian must defend the kingdom of Ithyria from a dangerous enemy and ultimately choose between her duty to the Goddess and the love of her childhood sweetheart, Erinda. (978-1-62639-329-5)

The Witch of Stalingrad by Justine Saracen. A Soviet "night witch" pilot and American journalist meet on the Eastern Front in WWII and struggle through carnage, conflicting politics, and the deadly Russian winter. (978-1-62639-330-1)

Night Mare by Franci McMahon. On an innocent horse-buying trip, Jane Scott uncovers a horrifying element of the horse show world, thrusting her into a whirlwind of poisoned money. (978-1-62639-333-2E).

Pedal to the Metal by Jesse J. Thoma. When unreformed thief Dubs Williams is released from prison to help Max Winters bust a car theft ring, Max learns that if you want to catch a thief, you have to get in bed with one. (978-1-62639-239-7)

Dragon Horse War by D. Jackson Leigh. A priestess of peace and a fiery warrior must defeat a vicious uprising that entwines their destinies and ultimately their hearts. (978-1-62639-240-3)

For the Love of Cake by Erin Dutton. When everything is on the line and one taste can break a heart, will pastry chefs Maya and Shannon take a chance on reality? (978-1-62639-241-0)

Betting on Love by Alyssa Linn Palmer. A quiet country girl at heart and a live-life-to-the-fullest biker take a risk at offering each other their hearts. (978-1-62639-242-7)

The Deadening by Yvonne Heidt. The lines between good and evil, right and wrong, have always been blurry for Shade. When Raven's actions force her to choose, which side will she come out on? (978-1-62639-243-4)

One Last Thing by Kim Baldwin & Xenia Alexiou. Blood is thicker than pride. The final book in the Elite Operative Series brings together foes, family, and friends to start a new order. (978-1-62639-230-4)

Songs Unfinished by Holly Stratimore. Two aspiring rock stars learn that falling in love while pursuing their dreams can be harmonious—if they can only keep their pasts from throwing them out of tune. (978-1-62639-231-1)

Beyond the Ridge by L.T. Marie. Will a contractor and a horse rancher overcome their family differences and find common ground to build a life together? (978-1-62639-232-8)

Swordfish by Andrea Bramhall. Four women battle the demons from their pasts. Will they learn to let go, or will happiness be forever beyond their grasp? (978-1-62639-233-5)

The Fiend Queen by Barbara Ann Wright. Princess Katya and her consort Starbride must turn evil against evil in order to banish Fiendish power from their kingdom, and only love will pull them back from the brink. (978-1-62639-234-2)

Up the Ante by PJ Trebelhorn. When Jordan Stryker and Ashley Noble meet again fifteen years after a short-lived affair, is either of them prepared to gamble on a chance at love? (978-1-62639-237-3)

Speakeasy by MJ Williamz. When mob leader Helen Byrne sets her sights on the girlfriend of Al Capone's right-hand man, passion and tempers flare on the streets of Chicago. (978-1-62639-238-0)

Myth and Magic: Queer Fairy Tales, edited by Radclyffe and Stacia Seaman. Myth, magic, and monsters—the stuff of childhood dreams (or nightmares) and adult fantasies. (978-1-62639-225-0)

A Spark of Heavenly Fire by Kathleen Knowles. Kerry and Beth are building their life together, but unexpected circumstances could destroy their happiness. (978-1-62639-212-0)

Venus in Love by Tina Michele. Morgan Blake can't afford any distractions and Ainsley Dencourt can't afford to lose control—but the beauty of life and art usually lies in the unpredictable strokes of the artist's brush. (978-1-62639-220-5)

Rules of Revenge by AJ Quinn. When a lethal operative on a collision course with her past agrees to help a CIA analyst on a critical assignment, the encounter proves explosive in ways neither woman anticipated. (978-1-62639-221-2)

The Romance Vote by Ali Vali. Chili Alexander is a sought-after campaign consultant who isn't prepared when her boss's daughter, Samantha Pellegrin, comes to work at the firm and shakes up Chili's life from the first day. (978-1-62639-222-9)